NOW
You say
YES

Published by
PEACHTREE PUBLISHING COMPANY INC.
1700 Chattahoochee Avenue
Atlanta, Georgia 30318-2112
www.peachtree-online.com

Text © 2021 by Bill Harley
Cover and interior illustrations © by Pierre-Emmanuel Lyet

Edited by Vicky Holifield
Cover design by Kate Gartner
Interior design and composition by Adela Pons

Printed in May 2021 by Lake Book Manufacturing in Melrose Park, Illinois, in the United States of America.

10 9 8 7 6 5 4 3 2 1
First Edition
ISBN 978-1-68263-247-5

Cataloging-in-Publication Data is available from the Library of Congress.

BILL HARLEY

NOW
You say
YES

PEACHTREE
ATLANTA

To Debbie Block
in all ways, always
—B. H.

Chapter ONE

"The barbecue ones," Conor says.

"I know," Mari says for the fourth time.

"I don't like the other ones. Especially not the vinegar ones. They're bad."

Conor is standing sideways to the rows of snacks, facing the aisle that leads away from the meat section. His head is down—he's not looking at her. He never looks at her. He's not looking at anything except his fingers, which are opening and closing like they're on the inside of a puppet and the puppet is talking. But the puppet is silent. It's the motion of the hand that fascinates him, that has always fascinated him. Especially when things aren't right.

And things aren't right.

"I can't find barbecue ones," Mari says.

"They have to be there. Edith's Original Barbecue." Conor's head starts nodding up and down.

She leaves him there and walks back up the aisle, hoping that someone put Edith's Original Barbecue Potato Chips in the wrong place. There are thousands of bags of different kinds of chips, but only Edith's Original Barbecue Potato Chips will do. She can feel things spinning slowly out of control, turning aimlessly like some asteroid hurtling out of the gravitational force of some solar system—but her job now is to find the right kind of potato chips.

"Edith's," Conor repeats, loud enough for people in the aisle to turn and stare at him. He doesn't stare back, because he's an asteroid too, oblivious to the planet Normal. The other people in the aisle have sighted him through their own telescopes planted firmly on Normal, and they have stepped back to readjust the lenses. A woman with a baked-on tan, decked out in a fancy pantsuit from Rodeo Drive, turns her cart and heads in the other direction.

"Edith's Original Barbecue Potato Chips with the taste of real smoke and peppery barbecue. Homestyle recipe. Ten ounces net weight," Conor recites from the hard drive of his memory. "Edith's."

"I know," Mari mutters.

There they are. Thank God. What idiot put the Edith's with the Lay's?

"Here," she says, grabbing a bag. Conor turns to her, takes the bag from her hands, and clutches it to his chest. Without a word, he makes a hairpin turn and heads toward the checkout line in fourth gear, ignoring everything around him.

Mari follows. She doesn't call to Conor to slow down. It would just attract attention and he wouldn't listen anyway.

The express line is six customers deep. There are too many people around and Conor is beginning to stim.

Stim. Stimming. Short for "stimulating," or "self-stimulating." It's what some people on the autism spectrum do when things get weird for them—which is pretty often. If you're not used to it, it's one of the most disturbing parts of being around someone on the spectrum.

People pretend to ignore Conor, which means they stare at him when they think no one will notice. Mari has seen this a thousand times. Right now he's pretty interesting, since he's muttering the slogan of Edith's Original Barbecue Potato Chips under his breath, holding the chips to his chest with one arm, and staring at his flapping fingers with the other.

It's times like this that make Mari want to shout, *"Excuse me. May I have your attention? This is my brother, Conor. He's nine years old and is on the autism spectrum. Call it Asperger's. He may seem weird to you, but he's smarter than you'll ever be. And yeah, he doesn't look like me. I'm adopted and he's not. Mind your own business."*

But that would attract more attention and be a bad idea.

Mari has many bad ideas.

Mari slips her backpack off her shoulder and pulls her wallet out of the back pocket of the pack, hoping she has enough cash to buy the chips.

"We have to pay for the Edith's Original Barbecue Potato Chips NOW!" Conor announces. Everyone in every checkout line turns and looks at him.

He has no clue about how he affects others.

Mari wishes she could care as little as he does about what others think.

Coming to the supermarket was now, officially, one of her really bad ideas, but she had to get him out of the hospital, and the Vons supermarket was just across the street. She's in charge of Conor, but she's anxious about her mom. The store is crowded, the line is long, and someone in front of them has decided thirteen items is okay in the express line. It's the woman with the baked-on tan. Perfect. Rodeo Drive Lady is checking out her phone while the cashier rings up her items and everybody waits.

"You can open the chips now," Mari says to Conor.

"No," he says, shaking his head. "They aren't purchased yet."

Conor's sense of rules is so strong, so literal, so by the book, that sometimes Mari thinks he would gladly push the button to blow up the world if it were in the rule book. On the other hand, if a rule doesn't fit in with the Official Rules and Regulations of Conor's World, there's no way he would follow it, even if it was a federal law and they'd send him away for life.

Mari's heart catches. "Conor's World." That's what Mom calls his grid, his framework, his understanding of everything around him.

"I can't eat them until they're purchased," he repeats. "They are still owned by the store until they are paid for."

Mari remembers when Mom set this rule: the day when Conor opened up four candy bars in the checkout line, which made perfect sense to do, since they were sitting there at eye level, asking to be opened.

"It's okay to eat them while we wait," Mari counsels.

"We should pay now," he says.

People look away.

If it weren't so annoying, it would be funny. If a normal teenager talked out loud like this, being "inappropriate," his friends would laugh at his brashness. It's funny because it's breaking a rule—you're not supposed to talk this loud in a line of people you don't know. It would be hilarious.

"Pay now!" Conor repeats, a little louder.

People squirm. Everyone is nervously trying to ignore both of them, which means they are staring even more.

"We have to wait," Mari says.

And then her phone vibrates. She takes it out of her back pocket.

It's a text from Dennis.

Get over here now.

Rodeo Drive Lady is still busy on her phone, watching the girl bag her thirteen items.

There are three other customers in line in front of them.

"Let's go," Mari says, taking the bag of chips out of Conor's hand. She puts the wallet back in her backpack and slips the pack over her shoulder.

"We haven't completed the sale!" he says, loud enough for half the store to hear. "We can't leave until we complete the sale. *Then* they belong to us."

"Mom needs us," Mari says. Holding out the potato chips, she turns and walks past everyone in line. She doesn't look at anyone. She's hoping it will work, and it does—like a dog tracking a rabbit, Conor follows the potato chips.

They're out the door and headed across the street to Hamilton Memorial Hospital, where their mom is on a bed with all sorts of tubes in her, and their mom's stupid boyfriend, Dennis, is waiting for them, acting like he has the right to order Mari around.

She hands the bag of chips back to Conor, who clutches them like some religious relic that will keep him safe from harm. She figures the people in the store—the customers, the cashiers, the stock boys—are glad to get rid of her and her brother.

Taking a bag of potato chips without paying seems like a small thing when your mom is in the emergency room.

Chapter TWO

Halfway across the street, the phone in her hand vibrates. Another text from Dennis.

> Where are you?

Mari doesn't like Dennis. She has never liked him, and what he's done in the past hour hasn't made her like him more. Dennis is a contractor. He does window replacements and is rail thin and squints every time he takes a drag off his cigarette. He does have a pretty good laugh—he leans back and his mouth opens and his Adam's apple bobs up and down. But most of the time he laughs at the wrong things. He hasn't moved into their house yet, but Mari is afraid he might.

"He's a jerk!" Mari had told her mom a couple of weeks ago. "All he does is smoke and eat our food and take up space!"

Her mom had just shrugged, her broad back to Mari's pleas while she washed her coffee cup in the sink.

Mari never understood what her mother saw in most of the guys who passed through their little house in East Los Angeles. For two years after Kevin left (Mari won't refer to him as "Dad," since that would honor him in a way he doesn't deserve), her mom hadn't seen anyone. She'd just thrown herself into raising her two kids, one adopted, one with autism, and both of them trouble.

But then it had started—one guy after another coming through the house, some lasting two or three days, some weeks, some months.

"I just need someone around," her mom had said one day. "To help out a little."

And a little was all she ever seemed to get. Except for Carlos, who was funny and had a new pickup. Mari had liked riding in it, high above the road. One day he'd slipped a Katy Perry CD into the player in the cab and at the end of the ride, he had given it to her. And then it turned out he had another family and Mari's mom was just a side project of his. Finally his *real* wife put her foot down and said, "Enough!"

While Carlos was in the kitchen with her mom, trying to explain himself, Mari had put the CD on the concrete floor of the patio behind their house and smashed it with a hammer.

That was the second time she'd broken something with a hammer.

She didn't want to think about the first.

Dennis often seemed annoyed that she and Conor were there. He made pathetic attempts at showing he cared about who they were and what they were doing. But even if he didn't seem to like them, Dennis brought her mom flowers, and no one had given her flowers for a long time.

For her mom's sake, Mari put up with him.

Until today. Mari was at her summer job working as a counselor at a day camp at the Rose Bowl pool when Dennis had called her on her cell phone.

"I'm picking you up in five minutes. Your mom's in the hospital. Be ready."

Before she could ask any questions, he'd hung up. When she met him in the pool parking lot, he already looked like a rat searching for a way out of the cage.

"We gotta go get your brother," he said.

Conor was at a day-care program for special-needs kids at the elementary school.

"What's going on? What's wrong?" Mari asked.

Dennis was smoking and Mari rolled down the window so she wouldn't asphyxiate in the gray cloud.

"Your mom's in the hospital. Something happened to her."

"What? What happened? Is she all right?"

"I don't know, okay? Something with her heart. She had them call me at work. So don't ask me any more questions until we get there, then we'll both find out. But you gotta go in and get Conor."

"But do you think—"

"I don't know, okay, Mari?" Dennis said, his voice rising. He looked at her, but the reflecting lenses on his sunglasses hid his eyes. He took a deep drag and let the smoke out slowly, trying to calm himself. "We'll find out. But now you gotta go in and get Conor."

All Mari could think when she looked at Dennis was the question her mom would ask when Mari was trapped in a jam, surrounded by ill-behaved people who didn't understand her. Or when Conor was stimming or staring off into space or had to have his way when her mom was busy, which left it to Mari to handle.

"Who's the grown-up here?" her mom would always ask.

She meant Mari, who was just fifteen, which was not officially grown-up.

Now Dennis should be the grown-up, but he wasn't acting like one. She shut up and looked out the window.

When the car pulled into Las Flores Elementary School, she got out and they buzzed her in at the door. Inside, she explained to Mrs. Gota that it was an emergency, that her mom was in the hospital. Luckily, she'd picked Conor up before, so the receptionist didn't blink, and Mari signed her brother out. He didn't ask any questions, which was a minor miracle. Until they got into the car.

"Where are we going?"

"Mom's in the hospital," Mari explained. "We're going to see her."

"What's wrong with Mom?" he asked.

"I don't know, okay?" Dennis exploded.

Conor responded in kind. "Why don't you know?" he shouted back. "Why don't you know?"

Routine and clarity are what Conor wants. *Not knowing what's happening* is a recipe for disaster, because *knowing* what is going to happen and where things will be and when they will be there is the most important thing in Conor's life. And that's hard for a kid like Conor, whose life could be a movie called *Uncertainty.*

"Calm down, Conor!" Dennis yelled.

Which didn't calm Conor down. At all.

"It's okay, Conor," Mari said, being the grown-up. "It's okay."

Although it wasn't.

Chapter THREE

Mari and Conor reach the other side of the street and head for the hospital entrance. Conor hasn't opened the bag of chips. They're still clutched to his chest, and it seems like he's waiting for some official acknowledgment of the proper ownership of the potato chips before he opens them. Mari leads Conor past the person at the front desk.

"Wait!" the woman calls.

Mari turns and points to the *Visitor* sticker on her shirt. They're official. Mari is not used to feeling "official" and she relishes showing she is. Conor doesn't notice any of this. Then they're on the elevator, going down one level to the emergency room.

"I haven't eaten any," Conor says to himself, or to anyone who would listen. "We haven't purchased them yet."

As they go by the check-in desk, a nurse raises her head and gives them a long look, following Mari as she leads Conor through the swinging doors and down the hall to her mom's room.

And then everything slows. Mari's mind is making a hundred connections a second as she takes in the scene. There are two doctors and a nurse and an orderly in the doorway. And Dennis, who is looking at the floor. Everyone else is just standing there, like they are taking a break or something.

Why aren't they in there taking care of Mom?

Then they all look up at once, like a herd of deer, or dumb cows. Their eyes rest on Mari and she knows.

Mom is dead.

They all take a step forward like the same herd of mute animals and hold up their hands as if to keep her from seeing.

"Where's Mom?" Mari asks, although she knows. She tries to push through the group, toward the door, toward where her mom is lying on the bed so they can make her well.

Dennis grabs her and tries to hold her back.

"No!" she says. He releases her and she walks in by herself. Conor stands still, unmoving in the hallway, avoiding all the grown-ups who might want to touch him and his potato chips.

Now Mari is in the room, standing by the bed, and her mom's face is turned away from her. They've got the sheet pulled up to her chest and there are tubes running in her arms and in her nose.

"Mom," she says. "Mom."

Mari steps forward, closer to the bed. She reaches out with her left hand and touches a lock of hair that has fallen across her mom's ear. It's damp. She curls it in a finger and gives it a little twist.

Wake up. Wake up.

"Mom," she whispers.

And then there's a nurse by Mari's side, resting a hand on her shoulder. The woman doesn't say anything for a whole minute. It's the kindest thing anyone could do right now—just put a hand there quietly and give her some time. Mari looks at her mom and waits for tears to come, but there aren't any.

She's aware of feeling nothing—like her whole being has shut down.

After a few moments, the nurse leads her out of the room, past the doctors. Dennis is standing there with his jaw set in granite. Conor is still clutching the bag of potato chips, unopened.

"Mari," Dennis says, "you gotta take Conor out in the waiting room. You stay there and wait while I talk to the doctors." He is trying to sound tough and authoritative, but he is really pleading with her. He knows there's no guarantee of Mari and Conor doing anything he asks.

She walks down the hallway, past the desk, and the same nurse is looking at her. Conor follows Mari like a puppy. No one has said anything to her about what has happened.

If no one says it aloud, maybe it hasn't happened?

They sit on the uncomfortable chairs forever, waiting. Mari opens Conor's bag for him, and he begins to work on the potato chips. Evidently, in Conor's World, if you hold something long enough, it becomes yours whether you've paid for it or not. He takes each chip out of the bag, one by one, holds it up three inches from his eyes to examine it closely, turning it around on its edges. Then he carefully places the entire chip into his mouth and bites down.

"I like the crunch sound it makes when my mouth is closed," he announces.

Mari is numb. She's not even sure her heart is beating. She's not *in* a cloud—she *is* a cloud—insubstantial, floating and separate from the earth and the sky and the waiting area. People are talking all around her. The woman across from her is breathing like Darth Vader and Mari wonders if she's going to die too, right there, even before they get her into a room.

Conor doesn't know.

He knows Mom is in the hospital bed and there's something wrong, but he doesn't know that she's dead.

Dead.

Passed.

Not here.

Gone.

She thinks all those things in a flash, but it still doesn't sink in. What sinks in is that Conor doesn't know. Will he understand?

Who's gonna tell him?

"Who's gonna be the grown-up?" her mother asks her.

Mari gets tired of waiting. Maybe it's been five minutes. It feels like an hour. Conor is completely focused on the chips and she knows he'll stay there. She gets up and walks down the hallway. Just as she is about to turn toward the room her mom is in, she hears Dennis's voice. He's right around the corner.

"I know, I know," he's saying.

Mari pokes her head around the corner and sees him standing in the hallway, phone to his ear, his back to her. His jeans are drooping down because he doesn't have any hips and his T-shirt is riding up and she can see his underwear.

Under Armour. That's what she notices.

And the tone of his voice.

"No friggin' idea.... No. None.... Who knows? I mean, they asked me who's gonna sign the papers. Am I supposed to do that?"

And then his voice takes on a tone of urgency, of desperation.

"Not me. I didn't sign up for that. No." He lets out a burst of air that's part laugh and part disgust, shaking his head. "No.

The girl's a friggin' pain in the ass, a real loser. She don't like me. And the boy, Conor—he's not right. He's crazy. I can't handle them.... How should I know who'll take them?"

And then Mari's a cloud again, floating, alone. All the sound around her recedes and she pulls her head back around the corner. Her heart is beating like a hammer and she senses her breath going in and out, in and out.

Pain in the ass.

A real loser.

Not right.

Crazy.

Mari leans back against the wall. She is not thinking now. She is just knowing. It's not a mental process, not one thought leading logically to another, but an instant immediate knowing what she needs to do.

GET OUT. GET OUT. GET OUT.

Dennis stops talking. She hears his footsteps trailing off, headed away from her. Maybe going to sign whatever people sign when someone dies. Or going out for a cigarette. Mari peeks around the corner again and doesn't see anyone, so she walks down the hallway and into the room where her mom is. The room is still. Mari crosses the room and looks at her mom. On the stand by the bed is a plastic bag. In it is her mom's wallet and her phone and her car keys.

Mari takes the bag and slips it into her backpack. She kisses the top of her mom's head and leaves. She sees the hallway in front of her and her feet moving along the floor. Nothing else. All the way to the waiting room. Nothing else on either side.

"Come on, Conor," she says.

"What?" He is working on the broken potato chips now, but treating them with the same care and attention he gave the whole ones. Every chip is sacred.

"We have to go get the bus," she says.

Conor doesn't answer. He's too busy examining the broken potato chip. Mari is used to this, but it still drives her crazy. He's so good at not responding. It's like he's intentionally ignoring her. Except he's not. He's just busy with the potato chip.

"We have to go!" Mari raises her voice and Conor looks up.

"When is Mom coming?"

"Not right now," she answers. "But we have to take the

bus." She's hoping he doesn't ask any more questions, because he's much better at asking questions than she is at answering them, and she will run out of answers very quickly.

But for some reason he doesn't say anything. He leaps up, rolls the top of the bag down very carefully, and follows her out the door.

Into the great wide open, where there is no plan, no path, no promise.

Chapter FOUR

As they walk out of the hospital, Mari's mind races, imagining some official pronouncement about her mother. She assembles the cold facts she knows: *Stephanie Doherty Hammond. Born Stephanie Mary Doherty, on December 12, 1975, in Lynn, Massachusetts, daughter of Enid and Fred Doherty. Married to Kevin Hammond on May 14, 2005, in Los Angeles, California. Died August 17, 2017.*

Mari doesn't know a lot about Stef and Kevin before she came into their lives. She knows they met in California. Stef had come out from Massachusetts to be an actor, against her own mother's wishes, and Kevin had done the same, from outside of Philadelphia, wherever that was. He'd gotten some bit parts in movies and commercials. He sang and played guitar in a rock band.

Mari and Conor reach the street and turn left down the sidewalk. Mari is looking for a bus stop and hoping that she'll recognize the number of one of the buses. She knows the Target on Colorado Avenue where her mom worked is on bus route 256.

"Where is the bus stop?" Conor asks, walking alongside her, staring at the sidewalk directly in front of him.

"Not far," Mari says, though she's not sure. The hospital is on a busy street, but she doesn't want to wait at the stop right outside it.

Conor looks up. "There it is," he says, pointing across the street.

"No," Mari says. "That's the wrong one."

They need to get farther away. She sees another bus stop a couple of blocks up, in front of a park. She hurries in that direction, looking back to make sure that Conor is coming.

When they reach the intersection, she stops and checks out the numbers of the bus routes.

Bus 256. There it is. What she's looking for.

The bus goes right by the Target where her mom works. *Worked.* Mari looks up at the schedule on the kiosk. There's one in seventeen minutes.

Good. Conor likes the bus.

This kind of stuff is easy, Mari thinks—finding a bus route, getting to the parking lot, finding her mom's car. These are little practical problems that order her life five minutes at a time. She can do this. It's the bigger stuff that scares her.

Suddenly Conor takes off. He dashes across the street at an angle before Mari knows what's happening.

"Conor, stop!" she yells.

Oh no, not a runner!

That's what Mom called it.

"It's a runner!" she'd shout whenever Conor set off—down the street or through the mall or in a store—and then they would run too, hoping to catch him before he did something they were going to have to clean up.

Conor's already across the street, running diagonally toward the middle of a pocket park, tearing toward the playground.

It's a swing.

Conor will happily swing for hours. There's something about the motion of it that seems to calm him down, even put him in some kind of trance. Conor would keep swinging until he just shriveled up and died.

Died.

Dead.

Mom.

Mari crosses the street on the light and by the time she gets to the playground, Conor is sitting in the swing, pumping in a herky-jerky, straight-legged fashion, his body out of rhythm with everything. Finally he gets the swing going back and forth; his body relaxes and his legs begin to swing up and down in a fluid gesture, like he's one with the swing. It's as if his brain, which moves eighteen million miles an hour and makes connections no one else will ever understand, has just decided to take a twenty-minute vacation.

Mari sits on the bottom of the slide for a moment to consider.

What should we do?

Where can we go?

She stares at Conor as he swings—he looks like the sweetest child. There, swinging, content, he seems perfect.

Mari remembers once in third grade when she got into a fight at school. She can't remember about what—it was one of many. Banished from school for the day, her mom had come to pick her up. Before they climbed into the car, her mom held Mari's face in her hands. "You're a good kid," she whispered.

Mari smiled, and then her mom delivered the punch line. "When you're sleeping." Then she gave Mari a quick hug and a gentle shove toward the car.

Conor was a good kid. When he was swinging.

When he was confused or overwhelmed, not so good.

There were a million things to know and do, to decide, to figure out, and there was no one there but her. The grown-ups weren't around.

Mr. Alvarez, maybe? But what could an eighth-grade social studies teacher do?

What *could* an eighth-grade social studies teacher do?

Not adopt them. She knew Mr. Alvarez had four kids of his

own. He talked about them all the time. He couldn't adopt both her and Conor.

Mari tried to think of another family that might take them in. She was friendly with a few classmates, but the truth was, Mari wasn't really close with anyone. Not enough to ask to live with them.

They couldn't go back to the hospital.

Where could they go? Was there a place where she and Conor would both fit?

There was one place she definitely couldn't go back to. *Wouldn't* go back to. Especially not with Conor. The only place that would take her back.

The System.

The first time Mari had heard anyone talk about the System, she'd been sitting on the floor of a cluttered living room, playing on a worn rug with a broken plastic doll that wasn't hers, while the grown-ups talked over her head. She remembers feelings of dread and anxiety running from the pit of her stomach out to her arms and legs and back again.

"I hate to have her go back into the System," one of the child welfare workers had said.

"I can't take care of her any longer. She ain't right." Maggie Custer spoke as if Mari wasn't even in the room. Maggie Custer housed six foster care kids, all crammed into two bedrooms in her small house.

Maggie Custer was the one who wasn't right. There was never enough food to feed six children. You had to go into your bedroom at eight o'clock whether you were tired or not. If you made a sound, she came in with a wooden spoon and had you put your hands out, palms down, to accept your punishment. So finally, one night, as Maggie Custer was towering over her in the half-lit bedroom with two other girls watching wide-eyed, Mari had grabbed the spoon out of Maggie Custer's hand and flung it out the door of the bedroom.

Maggie Custer had turned to go after the spoon, but Mari was out of the bed in a flash, slipping past the woman's looming frame. She'd dived on the spoon, then held it out in front of her, like a five-year-old pirate or musketeer or Percy Jackson wielding a sword.

"Get away from me!" Mari had screamed. "I'll stab you!"

Which was pretty funny, really. Stabbed to death with a wooden spoon!

Funny now, maybe, but not then.

So back Mari went, into the System. Or actually, since she was already in the System (Maggie Custer WAS the System), she was just moved to another part of the System. Another house, this time for four months. And then another. Five, six, seven houses, all of her things stuffed in a black plastic garbage bag as she was shuttled from house to house. None of them home.

But then, somehow, she arrived at the house where Stephanie lived.

And Kevin.

At first they were just part of the System too. It wasn't until after three or four months that Mari realized she was still living there. Her stuff was in closets and chests, not in a black garbage bag. Even though she'd broken the plate-glass door.

And marked on the walls with lipstick. And spilled chocolate milk on the white rug. On purpose. While they watched. Even though she'd been picked up from school a half dozen times for her bad behavior, caused by an anger she couldn't control.

Stef and Kevin were part of the System too, because the System was big and wide.

And then Mari began to see there were accidents or openings, holes in the System, where people smiled and acted in a way that the System didn't expect them to smile or act.

Like the time when Mari dropped one of Stef's wineglasses. Kind of on purpose.

They were standing in the kitchen and it shattered on the tile floor. Mari watched Stef to see her reaction.

Stef looked at her and smirked. "Really?" she asked with a sarcastic grin on her face. Then she went to the closet, got out the broom and dustpan, and handed them to Mari. "Could you please clean that up?"

And so Mari did.

"I'm sorry," Mari said.

"I know you are, honey," Stephanie said. "It's okay. It's a stupid freakin' wineglass. They break easy."

Then a pause, then the punch line.

"But *I* don't."

Maybe they took her in because they couldn't have children of their own. Mari knew they had tried. And so their house was different from the other foster homes she'd been in. It wasn't a kid-holding bin, with children passing through so someone could pay their rent from the money they got for being a foster parent.

Mari kept waiting for the next foster kid to show up, but that never happened.

Stef and Kevin wanted a kid and couldn't have one. And so they had Mari.

And Mari stayed. And Stef became Mom. And Kevin became Dad.

And then Stef got pregnant. Which wasn't supposed to happen. But it did.

And that was Conor.

Chapter FIVE

Mari looks over at Conor, still swinging happily.

She knows two things. She won't go back into the System. And she won't let anyone put Conor in it either. He couldn't survive it. Especially alone, and they would be sure to separate them.

Where can we go?

She keeps coming back to the same answer.

Then rejecting it.

She can't.

She thinks of what she said.

"I wanted to hurt you. I hate you."

But it's the only place she can think of.

Whatever they do, wherever they go, first she has to just get them out of here. Far away. Before someone finds them.

Mari checks her phone for the time. "Five more minutes, Conor!" Mari shouts, using their mom's trick for giving him an order. *"Don't ask a yes-or-no question. Give him a number and he'll listen."*

After the time is up, Conor hasn't moved, except for back and forth. He's chanting under his breath. *"This little light of mine, I'm gonna let it shine, this little light of mine, I'm gonna let it shine, this little light of mine, I'm gonna let it shine..."* It's just the first line of the song over and over again. It's a song Kevin used to sing with his guitar, but the melody of the first line is as far as Conor ever gets.

"Conor, it's time to take the bus to Target. Just three more minutes."

Conor hops off the swing and strides, head down, toward the bus stop. Mari runs to catch up.

"Mom's not at Target," Conor announces as they walk. "She's in the hospital."

"I know," Mari says.

"She's not working. She's lying down," he says.

They stand at the bus stop, along with three or four other people waiting for one bus or another. Conor's right hand is beginning to open and close.

"I know," Mari says quickly, worried Conor is going to ask the question about Mom she doesn't want to answer. "But we have to go to where she works to get something."

"She was working, and then she went to the hospital. Now she's on a bed in the hospital."

"I know," Mari says again, "which is why we have to go to Target, since she can't go."

"Will we see Delroy?"

Delroy is Mom's supervisor. Delroy is about the only human other than Mom—and sometimes Mari—who Conor would let hug him.

"I don't know."

"When will you know?" Conor looks at his wristwatch like he's about to give Mari a deadline.

Just then the bus pulls up. Mari reaches into her backpack

for her wallet, removes her pass, and counts out enough change for Conor. As they start to board the bus, they're brought to a halt halfway up the steps. The man in front of Mari is searching the pockets of his worn suit jacket. His old brown wallet is in one hand, hanging open.

"I can't find my card," the man finally says.

The bus driver just stares out the front window. "If you don't have a pass or any change," he says, "you can't ride."

"I don't have it. It's gone," the man says softly.

"Sorry, sir. You gotta get off. People are waiting."

Mari is holding her own wallet in one hand, her pass and the change for Conor in the other.

"Please," the man says. "I'll pay later. I have to go home."

"Sorry, man. You gotta get off."

Mari can feel the impatience of the people behind her who are waiting to get on. She opens her wallet. She doesn't have much money—a ten and a five. No singles. The bus fare is $1.75. She pulls out the five and reaches past the man without a pass.

"This is for him and my brother," she says, holding the bill out.

The bus driver shakes his head. "I don't make change."

"I know," Mari says evenly and clearly. "It's okay."

She stuffs the money in the till and shows her pass to the driver, then she and Conor follow the man down the aisle of the bus. He sits on a seat, facing in, and she and Conor sit directly opposite him. The man nods at Mari—she can see he wants to say more but can't because of his embarrassment at needing help.

"I don't know where my pass is," he offers.

Now that Mari is close to him, she can see all the lines of age and hardship on his face, every one of them furrowed like the ravines and canyons north of LA on the 101 that snake their way toward the ocean. His hair is peppered gray, and short enough so that it stands up straight out of his head.

He's staring down at his shoes. They're sneakers, and they don't match—one bright orange and laced up so tight, you can't even see the tongue, the other a dirty-white old canvas sneaker, the sole pulled away from the toe.

He raises his head and looks at Conor, who's begun rocking back and forth a little, then looks back at Mari. Their eyes meet, and Mari nods and gives him a half-smile.

Mari gazes out the window. Even though she hasn't done anything yet, the fact that she's even thinking about doing it makes her feel like she's breaking the law or doing something illegal. And that makes her think other people will be able to tell that she is a problem.

Pain in the ass.

A real loser.

Not right.

Crazy.

She hates these words—they say more about the person who said them than the ones they're talking about, but they still hurt.

This feeling of being vulnerable—the feeling that everyone around her thinks Mari's up to something she shouldn't be doing—is heightened by Conor's presence. They don't fit together. They're brother and sister, but they don't look like it. She's long and lean, her face angular and thin, her hair straight and black. Hazel eyes. Conor's all curly and fair, with a round face, blue eyes, and pink skin that burns as soon as the sun touches it. More than once, when she's been with Conor alone, people have assumed she's his babysitter.

Which she is.

But also his sister.

Again she looks at Conor, who is rocking back and forth a little, staring at his opening and closing hand.

They're not normal.

What's normal?

Mari has never felt "normal." Six years in the System guarantees that you're not "normal." Conor isn't normal either, but he doesn't know it, somehow. In Conor's eyes, everything he does is reasonable. Mari wonders if there really is a Conor's World, or if it's just Conor's way of living in this one.

Mari turns back toward the window. She thinks of her mom, then pushes that out of her mind.

Not now.

Her mind goes back to what she's going to do. She has to decide.

But there's nothing to decide.

There's no other place. Only one place where both of us, together, have a chance.

She nods to herself. "Okay," she whispers. "Okay."

It's only a twenty-minute bus ride, and they're at the corner by the Target before Mari realizes it. Conor is already standing up, ready to head for the exit steps.

Conor's sense of space and distance and place is so acute, it's like something from a science fiction movie. Mari imagines Conor's interior map as big as the whole world—bigger even, expanding across the universe. It probably looks like some crazy diagram on a piece of graph paper.

The bus stops and heaves a long pneumatic sigh. The doors open, and Conor's out in a flash, heading across the parking lot toward the front door of the store, which is not where Mari wants to go. She wants to get in the car and drive away.

"Conor! Wait!" she calls.

Conor doesn't wait.

Mari breaks into a run across the parking lot, catches up with him, then gets ahead of him. She turns and stands in his path, so he actually bumps into her and stops, looking down.

"What?" he says, staring at the pavement.

"We have to go to the car first. To get something. Then we have to leave." She pulls the car keys out of the plastic bag in her backpack, holds them up, and dangles them in front of Conor's eyes.

Without a word he grabs them. Conor loves keys. He loves the sound they make. Sometimes when Mom was at the end of her rope with him, she would hand him the keys, and he would stop everything and shake them, listening to them clink back and forth against each other. Whenever they went on errands, she would let Conor hold the keys as they wandered through stores, parking lots, and hallways.

"He'll never lose them," Mom would say. "He's the Guardian of the Keys. More dependable than you or me."

Keys in hand, Conor turns and heads to the side lot, to the space where their mom has always parked because for some mysterious, secret, impenetrable reason, Conor told her it's the best place to park.

As they walk over to the car, Mari realizes that now is the time. She needs to tell Conor that Mom has died, though she's not sure if he'll realize what she's saying. Not sure what he'll do. Not sure how much she should tell him about what she wants to do.

But she has to tell him. For all his exasperating behavior, his stimming and apparent obliviousness to the world around him, he's too smart to be fooled.

Conor stands by the car, rocking back and forth, side to side. "Open the door," he says, handing Mari the keys.

"Conor," Mari starts.

"Open the door," he says again.

She unlocks the driver's door, clicks the key again, and all the doors unlock.

"Conor," she begins again.

"You have to hurry," he says. "There's a bus coming in fourteen minutes that will take us back to the hospital."

Of course Conor would have looked at the bus schedule, or maybe he's had it memorized for months, with all the stops and all the times. And he has a watch. He'll stare at that watch for half an hour—it's much more interesting and comforting than humans. He knows what the watch does, and it always does it.

A watch is a very reasonable thing.

Maybe she can delay telling him. If she could just get Conor home, then they could pack and put things in the car, and it would give her time to think about how to explain everything to him.

"Conor," she says, "we have to do something that Mom wants us to do."

"Mom's in the hospital," Conor says. "She went to the hospital so she could get better."

"I know. But I have to drive the car to the house to get some things."

"You can't drive. It's illegal and you're fifteen and three months and you haven't passed a driving test, which you can't take until you're sixteen, which you won't be for another two hundred and seventy-two days." Conor delivers this analysis of the situation in a flat voice, with no emotion—it's just the truth, a scientific observation not open to discussion.

He's right. He's so right about everything, and so *sure* he's right, his hand starts flapping, since the world isn't behaving as it should.

"I know how to drive," Mari says. "I've driven before. Remember?"

She has driven. A number of times.

It started almost a year ago. After a hike in the desert, east of Joshua Tree National Park, she had begged and pleaded with her mom to let her drive on an empty desert road. Her mom had finally given in and let her drive for five minutes, with Conor complaining in the back. After that, whenever they were far away from the city, where the roads were straight and there were no traffic lights or cars, her mom would sit in the passenger seat, letting Mari drive for ten or fifteen minutes down some empty secondary road, until they came to a busier route, where she would take over again.

The last time had been after a hike to Painted Canyon. Her mom had let her drive and then both she and Conor had promptly fallen asleep. It was late in the day, the car was warm, and Mari had driven on, unsure where she was heading, passing over the interstate until she found herself at a visitor center for Joshua Tree. She'd pulled the car carefully into the parking lot of the center, turned perfectly between the yellow lines of a parking space, eased the car to a stop, and put it in park. Then she'd touched her mom's arm.

"Where are we?" her mom had asked, jumping to attention.

"I'm not sure," Mari had said. "But I didn't wreck the car."

"Don't think this means you can drive anytime you want," her mom had warned.

"I know," Mari had answered.

But that was a straight road, with not another car around and an almost empty parking lot. This was different.

Mari opens the driver's door and climbs in the car. It's an old Honda Accord and the seat is worn and stained with spilled coffee. She puts the key in the ignition and turns it. The starter whines, the engine comes to life, and Mari puts her foot on the gas pedal.

The engine roars and one of the meters on the dashboard wheels around in almost a complete circle.

"Aaaaaah!" Conor is still standing beside the car, and he slaps his hands over his ears. "Too much gas! Too much gas!"

Mari takes her foot off the pedal and the engine winds down until it's just percolating, idling, awaiting further instructions. Her heart is hammering and she's taking short quick gasps of air.

The driver's door is still open.

"Get in the car, Conor, please. We have to go home."

And then, thank God, Conor opens the back door, gets in, and slides across the seat until he's on the passenger side of the back seat. Why does he do this without argument? Who knows? He straps on his seat belt and begins rocking back and forth. He's got his hands over his ears. "Put your seat belt on," he orders. "You have to wear a seat belt."

"I know," Mari says, closing her door and reaching back for the belt. "Okay. Okay. Okay." It's like a little prayer. She takes in one big deep breath and puts the car in drive.

Chapter SIX

Mari decides to practice a little—the idea of driving in traffic sets her heart racing. She makes a wide, cautious turn out of the parking space and down the aisle. The lot is mostly empty, and she drives around its edges, testing the gas pedal and the brake, creeping along the first time. The second time she uses a little more gas and takes a quick glance down at the speedometer. Twenty miles an hour. She uses the brake, then starts up again. Another car is about to cross their path so she brakes again, her sweaty hands squeezing the wheel, as if that's a brake too.

She wants to practice more. But she's afraid if she takes too long, someone will be waiting for them there, at home. She takes deep breaths and goes around the parking lot again, her turns becoming smoother, her foot on the gas pedal finding the point where the car accelerates, her other foot on the brake, finding the point where the car starts to slow without slamming her up against the steering wheel.

"Practice reverse," Conor calls from the back seat. She takes a quick look at him and sees he's still rocking back and forth, his hands over his ears, his eyes studiously staring at the back of the passenger seat.

"Good idea," Mari whispers. She remembers her mom looking at the rearview mirror, so she looks up and adjusts it until she can see out the back, then cautiously shifts the car into reverse. Then drive. Then reverse. Finally, after five more minutes of practice, she gulps, turns the car up the main entrance, and comes to an easy stop at the traffic light. It's red, so she keeps her foot on the brake, then realizes she's not sure she knows exactly how to get home. The light changes and she's not sure which way to turn.

I can't do this.

"Right," Conor says. "Right, then left at the second light,

which is Madison Street, and then you go 6.8 miles to Canela. Left on Canela and 1.4 miles to Oso Drive."

She pulls onto the street, gently puts her foot on the gas, and they take off, headed for home. As the car moves smoothly through the traffic, she takes a deep breath.

And thinks about Conor.

Tell him now.

Her mom had always told Mari things she didn't want to hear when they were in the car, her mom driving, both of them staring out the windshield, not at each other.

"Conor," she says in the gentlest voice she can find. He doesn't answer, so she goes on. "I have to tell you something. Mom died. She had a heart attack and she died."

Silence from the back seat. The traffic light ahead turns red and she pushes her foot down on the brake. The car bucks a couple of times, but she finally finds the right amount of pressure. She's still squeezing the wheel and her heart is still hopping up and down and she's panting like she's just run around the track in gym and can't catch her breath.

"You go to the hospital to get better," Conor says.

"I know." Mari's eyes are fixed on the traffic light over her head, but she sneaks a quick peek back at Conor again. He's still staring at the back of the seat, rocking gently. The light changes and she eases the car forward.

"We're going to Nana's house."

Conor stays silent. They come to the next light, and Mari has to get into the turn lane. There's a car ahead of her and behind her and one on either side.

How do people do this?

She glances at the driver in the car to her left. It's an older woman, and she's on the phone. She looks at Mari and frowns. Mari feels like she has a red neon sign on her forehead that is flashing "CAR THIEF!" She wants to crouch down low, but that would make her look even younger, so instead she straightens herself and tries to sit taller.

For once, Mari is glad she's tall for her age. She's always been aware of it, and hated that people noticed it, but now it's what she needs. She needs invisibility and being tall helps her now. What is the best way to be invisible? The best way is to be normal, just like everyone else.

So she pretends to be normal.

The light changes, and she has to make a wide turn, staying in the turning lane as she crosses through the intersection, onto the cross street, avoiding the car moving next to her on the left and the parked cars on the right. She makes it and straightens the car out in the right-hand lane. She lets out a breath she didn't know she was holding. No one's looking at her and she accelerates slightly. The engine revs for a minute, and now she's going thirty-five miles an hour. Headed for the next turn.

Then Conor speaks.

"That's a bad hospital. It didn't make her better."

Mari doesn't say anything. She doesn't know what to say.

They drive for another three or four minutes, and then Conor says in a matter-of-fact voice, as if to remind Mari of something she seems to have forgotten, "Nana lives in Massachusetts."

"I know," Mari answers.

"It's 3,125 miles from our house to hers."

That she didn't know. But she does now.

They turn onto Oso Drive and the traffic quiets down. It's residential, and there's no business traffic. One-story ranch houses are lined up next to each other as close as can be, so you can look out your bathroom window and see your neighbor's car parked five feet away. Since it's midafternoon, there's not much traffic. The sun is baking the pavement and the scrubby bushes in front of people's houses. Dogs are lying under the cars, looking for respite from the heat. Later in the day or on the weekend there would be activity—people out working on their cars or fiddling in the carports or talking to neighbors with beers in their hands. Kids kicking balls in the street. This is Mari's neighborhood, and she knows the feel of it. The one constant in her life, other than her mom, has been their house, which her mom kept after Kevin split.

Mari's not sure where Kevin is now—she thinks Thailand, which is the last place she'd heard her mom mention. She'd told her he'd sent an e-mail and said he was working at a bar on some beach.

"Friggin' loser," her mom had muttered under her breath when she read the message.

Mari wonders how long it will be before Kevin finds out about Mom, how much he will care. Mari sure isn't going to tell him. She feels the anger rise up in her again. Anger at Kevin for bailing on them, anger at Dennis for his dismissal of her and Conor, even anger at Conor for being such a pain. Anger at the word "loser," anger at the words "adopted" and "foster kid."

Mari feels angry about everything.

Anger ran like an underground stream through her. Her counselors at school had tried to get her to name it, to acknowledge it. And, for a while, after Conor was born, she had been less angry. Having a brother gave her a purpose, a reason to be. She was still angry at school, but not when she was a big sister. And then, when Conor's autism began to show itself, the boy she knew disappeared. Suddenly, almost overnight, he wasn't the smiling little brother who loved her. It was like he slipped into another world that she couldn't be part of.

She hated it when he went away. He was still there in the house, at the kitchen table, in the living room, in their shared bedroom, but gone.

Stupid Conor, she thinks. And then she feels worse because it's not his fault. It's the way he is.

When they pull onto their street, Mari feels even more vulnerable. What if someone who knows them sees her driving the car? She lowers her hands on the wheel and slinks down in the seat. Now it's a phantom car, being driven by unseen hands.

As they glide along, Mari's foot just barely touching the gas pedal, nothing stirs around them. When the car reaches their house, she casts a quick glance at the driveway next to theirs. Mrs. Cosamini. If there's one person Mari doesn't want to see, it's Mrs. Cosamini, who prowls the neighborhood like a one-person Neighborhood Watch, ready to stick her nose into anyone's business and fill her day with other people's lives.

There's no sight of her. Mari pulls into their driveway, lurching forward a little bit at a time until she hits the tennis ball hanging down from the carport roof on a string to mark how far to pull in. She'd seen her mom do it a thousand times.

"Conor," she says quietly, "let's get inside. Before someone sees us."

"We're not breaking the law," Conor observes. "We can be in the car, just sitting here. We're not doing anything wrong."

He should be a trial lawyer. He could make the other side cry with his logic.

"Right," Mari agrees, "but we don't want to explain how we got here without Mom."

"We got here illegally."

Mari gets out of the car and opens the back door. Conor has his legs pulled up on the seat, knees bent and heels pressing in against his rear end, while he vigorously rubs his temples like he's trying to massage his brain into some kind of realization.

"Where do they put Mom now?"

Mari feels a huge wave of confusion and sorrow rise up in her, through her chest and throat, and her mouth opens as if she's going to vomit something out, but it's only a huge swell of breath bursting forth over her tongue and into the air.

"Let's go inside," she whispers.

"Where will they put her if we're not there?"

He's not letting go of it.

"I don't know."

"Who knows? When will you know?"

"I'll tell you in a minute," she says. "Why don't you go play Minecraft for a while?"

Conor undoes his seat belt, scoots across the seat and out of the car. Mari unlocks the kitchen door. Conor pushes past her and goes into the kitchen, headed toward the den, where he'll flip on the computer and find Minecraft online.

As he walks through the door to the den, he calls over his shoulder, "It's illegal for a fifteen-year-old to drive to Massachusetts."

"I know," Mari whispers to herself. "I know."

Chapter SEVEN

On the spur of the moment, Mari runs back out to the carport, closes the driver's door, and opens the trunk of the car. Then she unlocks the cabinets at the back of the carport and begins to load camping equipment into the car—the two solo tents, two air mattresses, their old Coleman lantern, and their sleeping bags. As soon as she initiates the first part of her plan and gets some stuff into the car, she settles down a little and begins plotting the steps she needs to take next. There's a lot more to do, but the camping stuff is a start.

The camping equipment had been like a sedative for all of them—Mari, Conor, and Mom—something that calmed them all down. After Conor had started being the intense kid he now is, their mother looked for something, anything, that might moderate his moods and explosions. The world confuses him easily. Very easily. Sometimes he would completely lose it, and it would take forever for them to figure out what was bothering him.

It was exhausting. For all of them.

And then, when he was five, their mom had stuffed them both in the car and driven them to the ridge just north of Altadena, where they spent four hours hiking a trail. The entire afternoon went by without a single explosion of anger or sign of hyperness from Conor. Mom kept feeding him one peanut butter cheese cracker at a time until he stopped asking for them, and he seemed content just to be among the brush, through the eucalyptus, along the creosote bushes of the wash. At one point, he had run ahead, and then just stopped, fifty yards up the trail. He'd raised his head and turned slowly around and around, looking at the sky and tree branches then stopping for fifteen seconds to watch a turkey vulture circle on thermals high above them.

"Minor friggin' miracle," Mom had muttered. "Who knew you'd be a nature boy?"

That was the beginning. A few weeks later she'd chanced an overnight camping trip in Angeles National Forest. Conor had slept through the night, although the next day he'd insisted that he wanted to sleep by himself, which is why they bought another tent. Mari had liked the camping too, until the past year or so, when she got less and less interested in hanging out with her mom and her weird brother. She was less and less sure they were a family, and less and less sure she wanted to be in this family.

"Of course you don't want to tell anybody we're a family," Mom had said. "You're a teenager."

That had made Mari even madder.

Now she wanted the family back.

What's left of it now? Nothing but a "real loser" and a "crazy boy?"

She leaves the trunk open and turns toward the door. Before she goes inside, she takes a deep breath. She should try to talk to Conor again. Maybe she could make him understand what they needed to do.

Conor is on the computer in the den, staring at the screen, his fingers clutching the computer mouse.

"Conor," she says. "It's time to go."

He doesn't answer, so she takes a step closer to him and calls his name again, but still he doesn't answer.

His finger is frozen on the mouse and his head is starting to move back and forth. "No," he says.

"We have to go. It's okay. It's the best place for us." She puts her hand on his shoulder—a risky move, since she never knows how Conor will respond to being touched. The touch might break through his isolation—sometimes Mari can feel him relax and go to a different place in his head—or it might make things worse.

It doesn't work. He jumps up, not looking at her, and leaves the den. Before she can turn around, she hears the kitchen door to the carport open and shut.

Oh God, no, not another runner!

Not now!

Mari sprints through the kitchen, flings open the door, and steps into the carport. She looks down the driveway. He's not there. How could he have gotten away that fast? But then she hears a rustling behind her and turns and sees that the door to the dog crate is open. Conor's legs are sticking out. She sighs.

"Conor," she says, "please get out. We have to pack. I'm serious."

She should have known that's where he was going. The dog crate was left over from a rescue dog that didn't work out. They'd bought everything—dish, bed, collar, leash, fifty pounds of dog food—and then found out that Conor was allergic to certain kinds of dog hair. But by that time, the dog had chewed a hole in the plastic, and they couldn't return the crate. Then one day, they couldn't find Conor anywhere. They thought he had done a runner and were about to call the police, but Mari had found him curled up inside the plastic enclosure—a small safe place where he could go. To Conor, it was a secret fort.

Mari had thought it was a crappy place for him to be—if someone from a state agency had come and found a boy in a crate, they would've taken both Mari and Conor away. But Mom had seen it differently.

"It's his choice," she'd said. "He feels safe in there. At least we know where the hell he is. Who am I to argue?"

So the dog crate had stayed in the carport, and Conor retreated there when things got really bad. And although she is really annoyed, Mari realizes that having your mother die and your fifteen-year-old sister kidnap you and drive you across the country is pretty bad. Reason enough to make you want to hide in a dog crate.

Mari decides to finish packing, and starts to make a list in her head of what they will need. She'll put together some clothes for her and Conor. Ransack the refrigerator for whatever would travel. Look for any money she could find. Then, when everything else was set, and not until then, she'd try to get Conor into the car.

She finds the duffle on the floor of her mother's closet. She goes back into her room and sifts through her own closet and chest of drawers, just throwing in what will fit, leaving out any nice clothes.

But she pauses when she comes to the sweater. It's a Norwegian blue and white and red hand-knitted cardigan, with silver buttons and geometrically shaped reindeer on the shoulders and around the waist. She hasn't put it on for at least four years. It was buried in the bottom of the drawer and she hasn't even thought of it until she sees one of the sleeves sticking out from underneath a pink My Little Pony sweatshirt, another leftover from five years ago.

The sweater is way too small. She stuffs it into the duffle.

Mari goes back into her mom's room and sits on the bed. She pulls out the drawer of the bed stand, reaches into the back part of the drawer where she can't see, and feels for the jar. It's still there. She pulls it out, unscrews the plastic lid, takes out the bills, and counts. One hundred and sixty-four dollars. There would be one hundred and eighty-four, if Mari hadn't taken a twenty-dollar bill a couple of months ago. She'd wanted to go see an R-rated movie with some girls from school who had asked her if she wanted to join them. Mari was surprised— she usually kept to herself and other kids seemed to avoid her, so she was eager and nervous about going. She was afraid her mom would ask a lot of questions and not let her go, so she took the money without asking.

She'd felt bad about it ever since.

Now it doesn't matter.

Mari stuffs the bills into her pocket to put in her wallet later, then goes to the kitchen. She opens the fridge and begins to fill old plastic grocery bags up with anything that might work on the road—peanut butter, half a loaf of bread, jelly, wrapped American cheese, then pickles, which was ridiculous, but might keep Conor quiet for twenty minutes. She adds bananas and apples from the bowl on the table.

She lugs the duffle and bags of food out to the carport, puts the food in the cooler, then fills a big Ziploc bag with all the ice in the freezer and puts that in the cooler too. She loads everything into the trunk and closes it. Conor is still in the crate and not saying anything.

She decides to try again. "Come on, Conor. We have to go."

"I don't want to go," he calls from the crate. "We can just stay here."

They can't see each other, and Mari figures that's how Conor likes it—it's the perfect way for a kid like Conor to speak to another human being, where you don't have to look at someone else's confusing face.

"No, Conor," Mari says, trying to sound firm and not

pleading. If he doesn't agree to go, she knows she won't be able to make him. "We can't stay here. Nana's is the only place we can go."

"We can stay with Dennis."

"No!" Mari blurts the word out a little too loudly. She doesn't want to tell him what Dennis had said. *Not right. Crazy.* Conor has heard people calling him names, but somehow it still hasn't registered, and now is not the time to explain the difference between Conor's brain and the rest of the world. Now is the time to get him into the car.

"Dennis can't take care of us," Mari explains. "Only Nana can."

"Nana lives in Massachusetts," he says. "And we haven't seen her since August 8, 2014. That's nine days over three years. She doesn't know we're coming. We should call her."

Mari has thought of that. But when she thinks back to the last time she saw her grandmother, and all the time that has gone by since then without any contact, she doesn't trust a phone call. It would be too easy for Nana to hang up the phone, to say no, to call in the social workers. It's too great a distance. Their only chance is to show up in person. And hope.

"We're going to surprise her," Mari says.

"It's not a good surprise," Conor argues. "Some surprises are good. Like angel cake. Angel cake is a good surprise."

Mari looks at the ceiling of the carport. She fights back the anger rising in her.

"Conor, please."

There's no answer.

Fine, I'll just pack Conor's stupid clothes and stuff without his help.

She goes back into the house and into their bedroom, the small room they've shared for years, where she starts putting his clothes together. It's a simple task—he has five T-shirts that he likes to wear, one pair of jeans, and three pairs of shorts. She takes only two pairs of the shorts, since Conor is always complaining about the ones with the big pockets, saying they feel funny on his legs. There are other clothes in his drawer— piles of things Mom had tried to get him to wear, clothes he had rejected because of color, or design, but mostly because of feel. "This doesn't feel okay. It feels wrong," he would announce, and that would be it.

Mari hears a loud knock on the door by the carport. She freezes.

Chapter EIGHT

Is it Dennis? The police?

Mari doesn't move. Whoever it is knocks again, only louder. She remembers that Conor is in the crate, six feet from the back door.

Another knock, then a voice shouting.

"Stephanie. Stef! Are you in there? It's Rosie!"

Mrs. Cosamini.

Perfect.

Rosie Cosamini.

Her mom had called her "Nosy Rosie" one day, and the name had stuck.

Mari walks out of the bedroom and into the kitchen, her mind racing through a maze of possible stories she could tell. She is good at making up stories that aren't true to stay out of trouble.

She opens the door and Nosy Rosie Cosamini leans forward, trying to get inside. "Where's your mother?"

Nosy Rosie Cosamini is wearing the housecoat she always wears. She's a big woman, but after all the years she's been on the planet, her body forms a question mark, and her head juts out almost perpendicularly from her chest. Her mouth leads. In more ways than one.

"She's not here," Mari says, blocking Mrs. Cosamini's entrance.

"Her car's in the carport," the older woman says, trying to look around Mari and into the house. "She has to be here."

Mari can see Conor's feet sticking out of the dog crate, and she hopes he decides to stay quiet.

She thinks about saying her mom is out for a walk, but that won't work. Her mom never goes out for walks and Rosie Cosamini knows it. For a second it flashes in Mari's head to shout, *"She's dead. She died! Leave us alone!"* and slam the door. If only to see the look on Nosy Rosie Cosamini's face.

But something a little more subtle would be better. Something to buy a little more time. She knows that after the initial shock, Mrs. Cosamini might call the Department of Children and Family Services, or at least the fire department, which she did last year when Conor had accidentally started a fire in a trash can in the carport and set off the smoke alarm.

"I'm sorry, Mrs. Cosamini," Mari says, smiling and shaking her head. "I didn't say that right. She's in her bedroom trying to sleep off a really bad headache. She turned out the lights and asked me to not let anyone bother her."

"Is it a migraine?" Mrs. Cosamini asks. "It sounds like a migraine."

"It might be," Mari agrees.

"She doesn't have a migraine," a voice from the crate says.

Mrs. Cosamini jumps a little, turns and sees Conor's legs. She swivels her head back and looks at Mari, her penciled eyebrows raised.

"Conor likes to hide in there," Mari explains. And that's

good enough for Nosy Rosie Cosamini—Conor upsets her and makes her nervous, and she's happy to leave him in the dog crate. "It is a really bad headache, though," Mari adds.

"Oh God," Mrs. Cosamini laments, regaining her angel of mercy footing. "If it's a migraine, my heart goes out. I get migraines, let me tell ya. Is she sleepin' yet? Maybe I should talk to her about it." Mrs. Cosamini pulls on the pendulous lobe of her right ear, eager to share her nonexistent medical wisdom with a vulnerable person.

"Oh, that's really nice of you, Mrs. Cosamini." Mari reaches out and puts a hand on the woman's left forearm and gives her a soulful, earnest look. "She'll really want to talk to you. But could I call you when she gets up? She really wanted to be left alone. She said every time someone speaks, it makes the whole side of her face explode."

"That's what I'm saying," Rosie Cosamini moans. "Gotta be a migraine."

"She doesn't have a migraine," the voice from the crate says.

"Okay," Mari jumps in, before Conor can announce that their mother is dead. "She'll really want to talk to you, and I'll tell her. When she gets up." Then Mari shuts the door, leaving Nosy Rosie in the carport with Conor, Oracle of the Dog Crate.

Through the shut door, she hears Conor barking from the dog crate—something he does sometimes, maybe acknowledging that he knows he's in a dog crate and is pretending to be the dog they don't have. She stays out of sight for about thirty seconds, then peers through the window facing the carport. Nosy Rosie is gone. Maybe Conor's barking scared her away.

Then Mari goes into the den to turn off the computer. Whatever happens, Conor's not going to be playing Minecraft for a while.

But Minecraft isn't on the screen. There are no sounds coming out of the computer speakers—no explosions or beeps, no music looping over and over again as when Conor's characters wander from one place to another. Just silence. Nothing moving on the screen.

Instead she sees a map. Over the map is a jet-black circle in the middle of a bright yellow ring with a golden corona of light spreading out around it.

And in that instant the answer comes to her. She knows

how to get Conor at least halfway across the country. She has no doubt it will work. A word springs to her mind, a wonderful word her teacher Mr. Alvarez had used once.

Epiphany.

"It's a sudden realization," he'd said. "Like angels showing up out of nowhere."

Chapter NINE

The image on the computer screen is a solar eclipse.

Beneath the picture is a map of the United States with a broad arcing path running across it, a blue line tracing the center of the shaded trail from Oregon to South Carolina.

Open on the desk beside the computer is Conor's favorite book.

Astronomy: A Beginner's Guide to the Universe.

Five hundred pages of information, and Conor has absorbed most of it, even though it is far above his reading level. All about the dust tails of comets and the angular momentum of planets and the earth's magnetosphere.

Having taken in the information, he can now spit it all back out—one factoid after another—unconcerned whether anyone else is interested.

He'd started talking about the eclipse more than a year ago. He told Mari and her mom over and over again that soon a total eclipse would be crossing the United States and mentioned a million different places where they could see it. He'd calculated the closest place it would be to Los Angeles (Monmouth, Oregon, 920 miles) and when they would have to leave to get there.

Mom had said, "We'll see, honey. Probably not. I have to work."

"Don't say probably not," Conor had said, looking up at the ceiling. "Don't say not. Don't say we'll see."

He hadn't let go of it, and by February, he'd known enough about the eclipse to make your eyes and ears bleed. It was endless, him sitting on a stool in the kitchen, reciting the history of every eclipse over the past hundred years. And about exactly what would happen to your eyes if you stared at it. And what the birds would do, and how much the temperature would drop, and what the percentages were all across the country of having a clear sky. Which is why he'd settled on Rigby, Idaho, as the place they were going to see it.

Conor had his last full-blown meltdown about going to Rigby in April. Mari and her mom had to hold on to him for five or six minutes before he began to calm down. He'd tried to wrench a huge lock of Mom's hair out of her head, then kicked at Mari until she could get close enough to him so that his kicking didn't have enough force to hurt her.

"You said we'd see, and now you say yes," Conor sobbed. "Now you say yes. Now you say yes. Now you see and now you say yes."

"I know, honey, I know," Mom said, squeezing him and pressing her head to his chest. They were sprawled across the couch, all three of them in the living room, a tangle of arms and legs and tousled hair and wrinkled clothing and tears and snot and red faces.

"Now we see," Conor panted, "and so we go to see it."

"I'm sorry, honey," Mom said. "I should have just said no."

"Total eclipse...in Rigby, Idaho...is 11:33 a.m.," he choked out in between sobs and wails.

"No, honey," Mom said, holding him tighter.

"Jackson, Wyoming...at 11:34 a.m.," he offered, as if putting it off for one more minute would make a difference.

Finally the fit had petered out—Conor wiped his nose one more time and just walked away. No more mention of it. Like that—a switch-off in the circuit of mystery inside his head.

But this—his obsession with the eclipse—is something she can use. She goes back out into the carport and stands in front of the dog crate. Conor's legs are pulled inside.

"Conor...," she starts.

"No!" he calls out from inside the crate.

"Conor, on the way to Nana's we can go see the eclipse. You can figure out the best place to watch it. It's in four days." Even Mari knew the date was August 21. It had been fixed into her brain by Conor's repetition.

The Oracle of the Dog Crate is silent.

"Don't you want to see the eclipse?"

And then he answers. "One-eighteen p.m. in St. Clair, Missouri. On Interstate 44."

Mari has no idea how far out of the way that will take them, but she doesn't care. "Sure," she says. "Missouri."

It's quiet for ten seconds, and then Conor's head pokes out of the crate, followed by the rest of him. "We have to pack," Conor announces, standing up.

"I already packed."

"You forgot things," Conor says, pushing past her without another word. He dashes into the house before she can stop him.

She hears him up in their room, yanking open drawers and fumbling through the closet.

Fine. Let him think that, as long as we're going.

Conor shows up in the hallway with another duffle over his shoulder. He grabs the astronomy book, tucks it under his right arm, and heads toward the kitchen. Mari instinctively grabs him by the shoulder, but he hunches over and rips away from her.

"No!"

"We have to watch out for Mrs. Cosamini. We don't want her to see us."

"I don't care if she sees us," Conor says, lurching out the kitchen door. "She can't catch us."

As Mari leaves the house, she turns and looks around. The coffeepot is half-filled—her mom would have reheated it when she got home. The refrigerator whirs. The *Love Is Welcome Here* sticker is on the fridge.

Mari steps out onto the carport and locks the door behind her.

Conor is dragging something out from the corner.

The dog crate.

Perfect.

"We don't have room for that," Mari protests.

"Yes, we do," Conor answers. "It goes behind the driver's seat and I can sleep in it. We can buckle it in so we're obeying the law."

Mari thinks about telling Conor that disobeying the law by not wearing a seat belt is the least of their problems, but she keeps quiet. She has watched her mom weigh every possible argument with Conor, deciding if it's worth it. And she thought of her mom's line, a phrase she'd learned from Carlos and would deliver in a Boston accent: *"No vale la pena"*—not worth the pain.

There is enough pain already. And so the dog crate comes.

They get in the car—Mari alone in the front, Conor in the back behind the passenger seat. He puts his seat belt on and looks at the ceiling. Mari buckles in before she gets a lecture from Mr. Safety.

She looks around the car. Her mom's phone is lying on the seat. She realizes that if they need a phone—and they do—she'll have to use this one. Mari's, now stuffed in the trunk in her backpack, is limited in minutes and data—they can't use it as a GPS. There's a phone charger plugged into the adapter—the car is old and doesn't have Bluetooth or even a USB port. There's no satellite radio—just a CD player and regular radio, and eight or ten CDs her mom listened to over and over again, in spite of Mari's protests. It's a ten-year-old Honda Accord with 180,000 miles on it and it makes a weird noise when you turn it hard to the right.

The car smells like her mom. But Mom's not here and Mari is sitting in her mom's seat.

"You don't know which way to go," Conor informs her.

No, she doesn't, except to Boston. Or, more exactly, Lynn, Massachusetts.

So Mari does the sensible thing. She goes to the GPS on her mom's phone and types in "Lynn, Massachusetts." The phone is surprised they're going so far away and takes forever to come up with a route.

"We have to go through Missouri or Kentucky to see the eclipse," Conor warns her.

Two routes come up—the faster one is through Chicago. The other goes through St. Louis and is four hours longer—47 hours and 40 minutes.

She hands the phone back to Conor. "You navigate," she says.

"We go right out of the driveway," Conor says. "But you have to back out."

"Okay," Mari breathes out. She puts the keys in the ignition.

"It's ninety-two hours and five minutes until the eclipse," he says.

"Okay," she says again, and turns the car on. The engine roars. She realizes that she's got her foot down too far on the pedal, so she lets up on it. The car calms down, then she shifts into reverse and turns around like her mom does to look behind her. As she lightly touches the accelerator, Nosy Rosie Cosamini comes into view. The car moves on by her. Even though Mari is concentrating on what's behind her, she steals a quick glance at the woman and sees the arched eyebrows and wide-open mouth. Nosy Rosie is waving her arms and screaming words that are completely incomprehensible. Mari backs the car onto the street and turns, but too quickly. Suddenly the car is off the driveway and on Rosie Cosamini's yard. Mari jams on the brakes, but it's too late—she hears a thud.

"You hit her reflecting ball," Conor says.

Mrs. Cosamini runs up to the passenger side and beats on the window. "What are you doing? What are you doing?" she screams, her bottom lip quivering.

Mari puts the car in drive and it lurches across their own yard, over a bush, then onto the street, where Mari guides it back to a straight line.

In the rearview mirror she sees Rosie Cosamini standing in the middle of the street, her hands held in the air as if she's asking for help—or offering up a prayer to the universe.

And then they're off.

On the way to Boston. On the way to Lynn.

This is what pops into Mari's mind as they drive down the street—the first line of the nursery rhyme Nana used to sing to her when she was little, bouncing her on her knee. It was a song grandparents in New England sang to their little grandchildren.

Mari had been trying not to think of Nana, ignoring the question in the back of her mind.

Will she let us in?

But there's no other place to go.

Chapter TEN

"Route 60 to the 605 to the 210 to the 15. It's thirty-eight miles to the 15, exit—"

"Okay, slow down. One thing at a time."

Conor repeats the routes. Then he recites them again. Maybe it's not for Mari's benefit, though it's hard for her not to take it personally, like he thinks she's an idiot. She eases up the on-ramp—it's still rush hour and she has to stop at the light at the head of the ramp to wait to get on. Then they are on the highway with thousands of other cars, five lanes either way, all going somewhere.

Her hands are squeezing the steering wheel and her palms are sweaty. She's hyperalert, noticing everything around her, but her eyes are focused directly in front of her—she's conscious of all the other traffic but trying to ignore it while she stares at the lane straight ahead. Finally, after four or five minutes, she can't keep up the intense attention and she lets go a little. She pushes air out of her mouth, her lungs, her throat. As she relaxes, her foot eases up on the gas pedal and the car slows. Then she pushes down, slowly, gradually, until the car finds its place in the flow of the traffic. And she loosens up again—calmer but still alert.

She stays in the right lane, even though she has to keep braking for cars getting off or coming on ahead of her. She glances at people as they pass by—they're looking ahead or at their phones or in their rearview mirrors, but not at her, the fifteen-year-old without a license. No one's looking at her. They don't care what she's doing. When there's a big opening in the lane to her left, she accelerates and gets into the second lane.

I'll just stay in this lane. All the way across the country.

Not too fast, not too slow.

The traffic opens up. Working to keep in the flow, she glances at the speedometer. Sixty-two miles an hour. That's a good speed. Mari was always yelling at her mom to drive a little faster. Her mom sometimes drove faster than the speed limit, but it was still too slow for Mari.

Not anymore.

"Route 605, one half mile," Conor the Human GPS announces.

Mari merges onto the bigger road, then into the middle lane. She realizes that sixty-two miles an hour isn't fast enough. Cars are passing her on either side, and the van behind her is too close. She speeds up a little. When she feels herself in the flow of traffic again, she relaxes a little more. She's getting the hang of it.

Twenty minutes later Conor announces, "Route 210, one half mile." Mari thinks he could get a job recording his directions for some travel app.

They merge onto the 210, and now they're headed out of LA, straight east.

She sees a sign for Rancho Cucamonga. She's seen signs for it before, and always imagined Rancho Cucamonga as a big, beautiful Western ranch, with horses and cattle and cowboys. She loved the rhythm of the word—Cucamonga, Cucamonga—

and in her mind it had taken on some mythic quality. A magic place to go.

But now, driving through Rancho Cucamonga, it's just another place with signs soaring in the air telling her there is gas and food and tires and home goods and lottery tickets and cell phone plans. The Rancho Cucamonga in her mind isn't real.

Suddenly a California Highway Patrol car appears in her rearview mirror, very close behind her.

Its top light is on, spinning and flashing along with the lights in its grille.

She's caught.

She takes her foot off the gas, wondering what to do.

And just like that, the patrol car shifts into the lane to her left and speeds past, chasing someone or something else.

"Oh jeez," she says, putting her hand over her heart.

The speedometer levels off at forty-two miles an hour. Vehicles hurtle by her on either side, and the car behind her flashes its headlights, telling her to speed up. She presses on the accelerator, and the car, seemingly of its own will, finds the speed of the traffic again while she recovers.

For the next ten miles, she sees California Highway Patrol everywhere she looks. The "frequency illusion" is what Mr. Alvarez called it—like when you learn a word and then suddenly see it all over the place, or you find out your mother has a heart condition and suddenly you find out every person in the world has a heart condition. Or someone you know dies and then...

Conor is silent in the back seat. When she takes a quick glance back, he's staring at the phone, flicking buttons with his thumbs. She wonders what he's looking at but leaves him alone. Conor being quiet and undemanding is a blessing. They fly past one exit after another, past fast-food signs and Best Buys and Targets and La Quinta hotels and millions of people swarming like a hive, swirling around each other. The mountains are on their left, and the sun is beginning to lower behind them, shining through the back window.

"I wonder if we can see the moon?" she says to Conor.

"The moon set at 3:16," the Oracle of the Back Seat answers. *Thanks, Mr. Know-It-All.*

As they drive on, the traffic lessens a bit at a time, and then she turns onto I-15, heading north, over the mountains, away from Los Angeles. There's an accident on the side of the road with three California Highway Patrol cars around it. And an ambulance.

Her mom was in an ambulance five hours ago.

She shakes it off.

They begin to climb the pass and the buildings fall away, with manzanita and prickly pear cactus on the side of the highway, as the road rises and winds, turns and bends, higher and higher. As she comes around a wide curve to the left, she looks back and down at the clutter and spread and pattern of human life behind and below them, the exhaust of breathing and coughing and spewing she and Conor are leaving behind. She chokes convulsively. For a second she's afraid she's losing control, and then they're over the pass and a wide openness spreads out below them—it's the desert, and there's the highway snaking down, with an access road running alongside it.

But mostly it's just space stretching out before her.

They're on their way.

Chapter ELEVEN

Mari flicks on the radio and looks for a station—something with dance music. But the mountains hide the LA stations and here it's just religious stations and country music, which she doesn't want to listen to. The music is lame and doesn't have anything to do with her—she's not riding around in a car with the windows open drinking a beer and someone's hand on her leg, and she's not laughing.

The music isn't hers.

What is hers?

She doesn't remember her birth mother or know anything about her birth father.

"You don't want to go back and dig around," a social worker she trusted had said. "She was young. Her living situation wasn't good, and she knew she couldn't care for you. She gave you up. It was the biggest, kindest thing she could have done for you. You're going to get a new mom someday, and she'll be your real mother."

"Gave you up." What a weird thing to call big and kind.

Mari can't remember the first couple of places they put her—she was too young then. The first house in her memory was from when she was around four. Mari knows she'd be better off not to think about those times, but once in a while they show up in her mind uninvited—spending a night alone, or being hit on the hand again and again, or a having a big person towering over her and yelling. But here, on this desert highway, her mind takes off, releasing a cataract of thoughts and feelings and pictures.

Those people who had housed her (and that's all it was, housing) were all different kinds, all different colors. She knew more about them than she did about herself. After all the moving, she came to believe she didn't belong anywhere, with anyone.

But finally there was Stef, who became Mom.

Even though they didn't look anything alike.

Mari couldn't forget that she was adopted. It was like she came from some other planet.

"I don't belong with you," she had told Stef after a department store clerk had made some mention of how different they looked.

Her mother had pulled the car over to the side of the road. "Listen, you goofball," she'd said, holding Mari's face in her hands. "I don't care where you're from, but I know where you belong. Right *here*. So stop it."

So Mari hadn't mentioned not belonging again. But while she understood what her mom meant, it hadn't answered the question of who she was.

She reaches down to the pocket on the door and pulls up the nylon CD holder. It's unzipped and she holds it up on the steering wheel to find something decent.

She slips a CD into the player. A slow beat with violins swelling in the background. She recognizes the music right away, if not the name of the song. Mari had always complained about it whenever her mom played it.

Mari likes a driving dance beat, an insistent pulse that makes her feel alive—she likes to put in her earbuds and walk down the street or through the hallways at school and pretend like she's in a movie, watching the whole world move in time to her being.

Eject.

She looks at the next CD. Tori Amos. It's just a piano at first. Mari recognizes the opening lines, something about not wanting to be a boy. Beyond that, Mari has no idea what the woman is singing about.

And where's the beat?

Eject.

The next CD has a buzzing guitar and a guy with a crappy voice—he's barely singing and it's almost rap but it's too slow and he sounds bored.

Eject.

"You're not even listening," Conor says from the back seat.

He's parroting Mom.

Mari would always push the search button on the car radio again and again, not letting any song last longer than ten seconds, looking for something she could tolerate.

"Jesus, Mary, and Joseph," her mom would say. "Leave it somewhere for thirty seconds, will you? You're not even listening."

So Mari takes out one more CD and looks at it before she puts it in. It's a CD her mom had made, copied from somewhere else, and her writing in marker is scrawled on it. *Gull Power— The Gulls.* She almost doesn't put it on, because she remembers complaining about it, and her mom not letting her eject it.

"I know the drummer. It's my friend Carrie's sister," she'd said. "They should've been famous, like nationally famous. Five girls kicking ass. God, I loved that band." Her mom had gone on and on about getting into a club when she was underage and seeing them.

But Mari had always refused to listen to it on principle. If her mom liked it, then she didn't.

Mari slides the CD in. There are four smacks of a snare drum to count off, and then two distorted guitars pounding away. She's heard it before. Heard it, but not listened to it.

Her mom's not there, so she puts her finger on the eject button.

"Just leave it!" Conor shouts.

It's going to be a long trip. Mari imagines listening to this one CD for three thousand miles. She skips to the next track but it's no better.

> *Bloodred morning on a dark blue day*
> *No reason for me to stay*

The singer's voice sounds ragged and broken.

She hits the button again. At least this one has a steady beat, something you can dance to. But then that same voice comes on, the one that cracks when she gets to the top notes. Mari reaches to push the eject button.

"Just leave it," says the voice from the back.

So Mari leaves it, trying to figure out what her mom saw in this music. The singer spits out the words, a flood of language that is hard to follow. Mari only catches half the phrases, which don't seem related.

> *Random testing, random shots*
> *Blurred till you lose your yellow dress*

Clouds pile up like broken promises
Until the rain comes down

What are they talking about?

But she lets it play as they head up to Victorville. She remembers going to Victorville once—her mom had a friend there.

After she sees a fourth California Highway Patrol car, she recalls Dennis saying that the state police stay on the big highways. She wishes they could drive on a smaller road. Maybe there wouldn't be so many police cars on it.

So in Victorville, when she sees a sign for Old Route 66, she remembers that it follows the interstate. She takes the exit. Conor immediately sits up.

"What are you doing?"

"I'm taking another route," she says. "It's okay."

Mari takes a left and heads out of Victorville on a two-lane road, hoping that it turns to follow the highway.

"It's not okay. The big highway is faster. We have to be in St. Clair, Missouri, on Monday at 1:17. This will take too long. It's not okay. It's not okay."

"Just for a little bit," Mari says, digging in her heels. If she's driving, she gets to make some decisions, even if they aren't part of Conor's World.

"No! No!" He starts wagging his head.

"Too bad!" she says, pissed off now. She tunes Conor out like he so often tunes her out. She turns up the music, even though she doesn't want to listen to it. It's a big drumbeat and the singer is shouting out dozens of words Mari can't catch. Conor starts chanting, "Wrong way, wrong way, wrong way," but in time to the music. Mari turns the CD up even louder as they drive along. Conor keeps up his chant—"wrong way, wrong way, wrong way"—and in retaliation Mari starts chanting along with him, louder and louder until she's singing it out louder than Conor. Suddenly her brother falls silent and she hears the woman singing, her voice rising with each line, and the rest of the band, two, then three, then four voices joining in, one by one until they're all singing over and over again—

Sometimes I feel better
Sometimes I feel better
Sometimes I feel better

And then all of them shouting:

When I scream!

The song finishes. "I'll get back on the highway next chance," Mari says.

"Barstow," Conor says from the back, and she realizes that he's crawled into the dog crate, where it's safe. Safe from his sister yelling and going the wrong way and the California Highway Patrol.

"Okay," she says.

"I'm hungry," he says.

They drive for a while, and then he calls out from the dog crate. "I want track ten. I want the moon song."

"What?" Mari asks.

"Track ten. Track ten on the CD."

She skips the CD to track ten. The song starts and it's one guitar strumming. The singer chants "hey, hey, hey, hey" over and over again and so does Conor. When it seems like that word is going to be repeated forever, the song shifts gears and swings into a rising progression, with the drums settling into a relaxed, comforting beat. The singer goes into the chorus and so does Conor, in a horrible, out-of-tune voice, the rest of the band joining in on the repeated lines.

> *I wanna live on the moon*
>
> *Don't you?*
>
> *(Don't you?)*
>
> *'Cause I need a place with room*
>
> *Don't you?*
>
> *(Don't you?)*
>
> *Don't tell me we can't breathe*
>
> *Don't say you don't believe*
>
> *Don't say it just can't be*
>
> *I wanna live on the moon*
>
> *With you*
>
> *With you*

The song doesn't knock Mari out, but Conor is singing and has stopped complaining, so she leaves it on. Just the fact that the word "moon" is in the song seems to be enough for him. When the song is over, he asks for it again, so she pushes repeat and he sings along in his out-of-tune, flutey little-kid voice. Mari glances in the rearview mirror and sees that he has climbed out of the dog crate and is strapping himself into his seat.

So she plays track ten again.

Chapter TWELVE

Barstow's a desert town—the main street's a four-lane road with red clay-tiled roofs and run-down motels sprinkled among truck dealerships and taquerias. The train tracks run along one side, and Mari can see the interstate off to the other side.

"I'm hungry," Conor says again. So is Mari, and when she finally looks at the gas gauge, she sees it's touching the red line. Her teeth clench. What if she hadn't noticed it?

She pulls carefully into a Valero gas station. Trying to stay away from anyone who might give her a second look, she negotiates the car alongside a pump on the far side of the station, where no one else is filling up.

"You stay in the car," she says to Conor. "I'll get the gas."

"I want food from the store," Conor announces.

"We've got food in the back," Mari answers.

He doesn't listen. "I'll get food," he says.

"No, Conor," she warns. But he's already opening the door and getting out. He walks with his head down toward the mini-mart inside the station. She wants to stop him but decides to fill up with gas first. This is going to be tricky—it's something she hasn't done before, even though she's seen her mom do it a million times. She realizes she's parked the car on the wrong side of the pump and has to put the car in gear, back up, and then go forward to get on the other side.

How to pay? Go in and pay the attendant with cash? Using a credit card could get her tracked—what if Dennis or Nosy Rosie has the police looking for her? Still, it's better to use the card now, before someone decides to shut it down. So she fumbles through her mom's wallet and finds a credit card. Mari pushes it into the slot and nothing happens. What's wrong? She tries again, flipping the card from one side to another, until she notices the question on the screen—*credit or debit?* She guesses and pushes the credit button. The screen asks for her zip code, and she sighs in relief—a question she can answer!

The pump whirs to life.

Lift nozzle. Choose grade. Begin pumping.

She sticks the nozzle in the feeder tube of the tank and squeezes the handle. The numbers reel upward on the display screen. Evidently, nobody has reported the card missing.

Who would report it?

Does anybody even care that she's driving across the country? That she's taken the car? That she's kidnapped her brother?

Will Nana care?

Will she open the door for them?

Mari fills the tank, puts the nozzle back, and pushes No when the screen asks if she wants a receipt. She feels a small surge of pride and triumph that she's solved this problem. Then she goes inside to see what mess Conor has wrought.

He's standing at the counter with three bags of Edith's Original Barbecue Potato Chips, a bag of Tostitos, and two bananas. He hasn't put any of them down and the guy behind the register is eyeing him with a frown on his face.

"My sister has the money," Conor says.

The guy's somewhere in his twenties, with a razor-thin face and a weird little jazz-guy goatee and fuzz under his bottom lip, like a woolly bear caterpillar. Tats of dragons and swords run up and down his arms, and he's wearing a belt with a buckle the size of a pancake. It says *Chick Magnet*. When Conor points at Mari, the guy's frown turns into a smirk and spreads wider across the narrow angle of his face.

"Your sister?"

"Yes," Conor says, looking at the floor.

The Chick Magnet stares at Mari, then glances out at the car.

"Where's your mom?"

Mari takes the measure of this dubious gatekeeper and figures he's not exactly the voice of authority, and definitely not the California Highway Patrol, although he might have encountered them once or twice. So she takes a chance.

"She sent me out with my brother to get gas and a snack," she says. "She's sleeping one off. I'm just doing what she tells me."

The Chick Magnet gives Mari the once-over, then a little wink, which she ignores.

"You from around here?" he asks.

"No," Mari answers, cool as can be. "Just staying at the motel up the street."

Chick Magnet nods and takes the card. It's under fifty dollars. She doesn't have to sign. He holds out the card, but when she reaches for it, he pulls it back and fixes his red-rimmed gray eyes on her. "You need anything else, you let me know."

Mari snatches the card. "Thanks, I will." She grabs two of the bags of chips and the bananas out of Conor's arms, turns, and heads out the door with Conor on her heels. They get to the car and Conor climbs in the back, where he immediately rips open the bag of chips he's holding. As Mari opens the driver's door, she looks back across the plaza and sees the Chick Magnet staring out the window at her. She smiles and waves.

Something in Mari reacts viscerally to the man's look. Her whole body cringes.

"Creep," she mumbles, then climbs into the car and dumps the food onto the passenger seat. She starts the motor, feeling a little more comfortable with what she's doing, and pulls back enough to make the turn onto the road. Before she shifts into drive, she looks back at Conor, who is turning a potato chip contemplatively in his fingers.

"Only one bag of chips at a time. You'll get sick if that's all you eat."

"I got a banana," he says. "Bananas have potassium."

"No more chips for five hundred miles," she says. She feels like her mom. Being the grown-up.

A mile up the street, she pulls onto Route 40. The sun is starting to set, and the shadow of their car is in front of them, racing away from the sun into the darkening sky that opens up ahead. She has no plan except to move on. Drive until she can't anymore. Find a place to stay. Get across the country as fast as she can before someone or something catches up with them. Hope that Nana has forgotten, or forgiven, or that her heart is bigger than Mari would dare hope for it to be.

Has someone called to tell her that her daughter has died? Had Stef and Nana spoken since that last visit, three years ago? If so, Mari didn't know about it.

The first time she met her grandmother—her mom's mom—Mari was seven. Enid Doherty had come for her first visit to Los Angeles. It was her first trip to California, though Stef had traveled back to Massachusetts with Kevin and Mari when her dad had died.

"Call her Nana," her mom had said to Mari right before they were to meet. "She'll like that."

Shy and unsure, Mari couldn't look the older woman in the eye when the newly adopted grandmother came in the door. Keeping her eyes on the floor, Mari had mumbled, "Hi, Nana." When her grandmother responded, Mari snuck a glance up into her face and saw it smiling back at her.

And that's when she saw the brooch, which she didn't know was called a brooch until later. A piece of jewelry, an oval a little smaller than an egg. It was pinned to the woman's dress, just off her left shoulder, with a lacework of gold circling the edges, and a translucent stone shimmering with clouds of green and blue. Instinctively, impulsively, forgetting she was supposed to be making a good impression, Mari reached out to touch it. To try to understand it, to see if it was real.

"What is that?" she asked.

And Stef's mom, Enid, now Nana, had knelt down. "It's an opal, sweetie. With gold around it, of course. Isn't it beautiful?"

Mari nodded, fingering the brooch on the woman's blouse, the filigree of gold threads twisting around each other in a braided halo. The opal glowed in the middle of the golden circle.

"Where did you get it?"

"Why, how funny that you ask," she said in her Boston accent, stretching out some words and cutting off others. "I got it from my grandmother. *My* nana. She brought it when she came from Ireland. And when I turned eighteen, she gave it to me."

Mari's heart leapt, as did her mind—making the connection immediately. When she was eighteen, it might be hers. If she was good. And then one day she'd be a grandmother with a granddaughter, and...

"It's so pretty," Mari said.

"It is. I feel prettier just wearing it. It means the world to me." She touched the brooch with her fingers. "I wear it here, where I can feel my heart beat."

And then Enid, now Nana, sat down on a chair in the kitchen and pulled Mari onto her lap. As best she could, she started to bounce the girl on her knee. But Mari was seven, and it was all the old lady could do to get her up and down at all.

In time with the bounces, Nana began to chant a singsong melody, her voice cracking and breathy with effort:

"On the way to Boston,
On the way to Lynn.
Look out, little Mari,
Or you might fall in!"

On the last word, the woman opened her knees and let Mari fall between them.

Before her feet could hit the floor, Mari grabbed ahold of the woman's thighs and screeched in delight, her tough-girl coolness evaporating in the play-party game meant for three-year-olds. She looked up at the smiling face—the lined, drawn face of her Irish grandmother.

"Do it again!" Mari said.

The headlights show up more brightly on the road as it grows darker and darker. The beams don't reach very far ahead, maybe fifty yards—just enough to see where she's going for the next ten seconds...and then the next ten seconds...and so on. Conor is asleep, and the Gulls CD is playing. The singer's voice floats over the sound of the car engine and the whine of the tires on the road, over the miles as the Honda speeds along.

The speedometer registers seventy, then seventy-five miles an hour.

Then something the woman is singing catches Mari's attention and she pushes the button to start the song over again.

It's slower than the other songs—there's a guitar strumming alone, and then she starts singing, but barely—she's almost just speaking the words. That's what catches Mari's attention. She gets every word.

> *They put you in the ground*
> *They turned to go*
> *I didn't make a sound*
> *No one would know*
> *No one would know*
> *They washed their hands of it*
> *Nowhere that I could fit*
> *I climbed into a tree*
> *Up where no one could see*
> *No one could see*

And then the voice is singing again, and the contrast between the speaking and the singing makes Mari's breath catch.

> *Branches like a ladder to the sky*
> *No wings, no way to fly*
> *The only thing that I could do*

Was climb back to you

Climb back to you

I'm always climbing

Back to you

The singer has lost someone—that much Mari understands. They've been buried. She starts the song again and listens carefully to the chorus. Her whole body turns electric as the singer sings about being lost and distant and blind, and then somehow, how it's all right, too.

Mari's being shakes with the overwhelming feeling that someone is singing directly to her—making up words for the moment she's living.

With the music playing and Conor sleeping silently in the back seat, the stars come out above her and the oncoming headlights rush to meet her and disappear behind her.

And then, suddenly, surprising herself, she begins to sob.

The coughs and gasps roll up from deep inside her, her hands on the steering wheel, her foot staying steady on the accelerator as if it belongs to someone else. She sobs at the thought of never seeing Mom again, at how she didn't say goodbye, at how cold the hospital was. How clueless and stupid the adults were—all of them standing around in the hallway, chatting like it was some math problem they were discussing. She sobs, thinking of how Dennis reduced her and Conor to nothing—to a few words: *pain in the ass, loser, not right, crazy.*

And she sobs because the only person who kept her and Conor safe in a world that was rejecting them is gone. Mari sees that she had been alone before, but that was when she was little and she didn't know she was alone. She'd always thought there must be someone out there if she could only find them— someone who knew the rules, who would take care of her, who knew the way things were supposed to be. And then Mari had found that person.

She wipes her eyes. But the tears keep coming.

Now she's alone, except for the kid in the back seat, who she is somehow instantly responsible for.

What if she dropped him off somewhere—at some childcare agency, a police station—and just drove away? The trip would be easier without Conor, or at least faster.

No. That would just make everything worse, and she wouldn't be any different from all those people who had let her down before, who had promised something, even unspoken, that they never delivered on.

Where would they bury Mom? Would Nana care that her daughter had died? If Mari hadn't done what she had done, would Nana have still been in their lives? Could Nana have saved Mom?

"Oh no, Mom," she wails. Conor sleeps.

Mari drives on through the night, not knowing what else to do but keep going across the desert in the dark, headlights reaching out to just beyond the moment she is in.

Somewhere around three in the morning, knowing she needs to pull over, she sees the sign: "Grand Canyon National Monument—93 miles."

It reminds Mari of something her mom had told her only last week.

Chapter THIRTEEN

Mom had cornered Mari in the kitchen—backing her into the counter and tapping her chest with her finger. "You know what we're goin' to do?"

At first Mari was afraid she'd done something wrong, but realized by the smile on her mom's face that it was something else. "What?"

"Where do you think we're goin'?" Her mom's thick Boston accent was increasing as she became more animated.

And then Mari figured it out. A big grin broke across her face too. "Really?"

"Really. The Grand Canyon. I ain't going to say I promise.

We're just doing it. And I'm not even going to tell you the day."

Mari couldn't speak.

"I ain't promising," her mom said. "I'm swearing on a stack of Holy Bibles."

This trip had been a long time coming. When Mari was ten, they had watched a special on the Grand Canyon. Her mom had told her seeing the Grand Canyon was a dream of hers, even when she was a kid back in Massachusetts, but that she had never had the chance to go. Seeing the light in her mom's eyes when she talked about the place, and wondering at the mystery of this wide, deep, millions-of-years-old canyon, Mari had decided it was a dream of her own, too. A dream they could share.

But every attempt they made failed. Once, her mom had asked for four days off and had even made a reservation at a hotel with a pool. And then their car had needed a new water pump, so they'd had to cancel the trip. The next time, the refrigerator broke, and the time after that, Mom had to use her vacation days because Conor was sick.

Her mom had promised they would go later. But they never

had. When Mari was really mad at her mom, she would throw it in Stef's face, like she was letting both of them down.

And then her mom had brought it up again just last week. This time it was going to happen. And Mari had believed her.

So when Mari sees the sign for the Grand Canyon, she knows they're going. For her mom. To say goodbye. But she's afraid if she tells Conor about the detour, he'll lose it. Mari decides if she could just get there tonight, and be there in the morning, it would be too late for Conor to object. She'll keep driving. Just two hours more.

But as soon as she decides to keep driving, a wave of exhaustion sweeps over her. Her eyelids grow heavier and heavier, and she finds them closing, then opening again. Once, the car drifts across into the passing lane. She shakes herself awake, rolls down the window, and hunches over the wheel, trying to stay focused, but her whole body sags with the weight of the past twenty-four hours.

She sees a sign for a rest area.

"An hour," she says out loud. "Just an hour, and then I'll keep going."

She steers into the rest area. It's just a small pull-off, with a cinder-block building for the restrooms. No one else is there. She pulls into a parking space, turns off the engine, and the silence of the night fills the car. Her mind and body are buzzing. She adjusts the seat, leans back, and closes her eyes.

"Just an hour," she whispers to herself.

"Mari, you have to wake up! Now. You wake up now. We have to go."

She opens her eyes to find herself staring at the car ceiling, Conor's face hovering over her, crusty-eyed, hair turned in on itself like it had been in the spin dryer.

She raises her head and looks out the car window. Then she remembers pulling over to the rest area. It's morning. The temperature has dropped overnight and she's freezing. A cold tangerine sun peeks over the horizon, a red line on either side, and the sky is a deep blue, like it hasn't woken up yet either. God, she feels sore.

She's lucky—it seems that no one else stopped here. Including any police.

"Stupid, stupid, stupid," she mutters to herself as she climbs out of the car.

With barely a word, they troop off to the restrooms. They make a couple of peanut butter sandwiches and they climb back into the car and Mari drives. She has her plan in mind, but doesn't want to mention it to Conor. Not yet. And thankfully, he falls back asleep, and she has a chance to get to the Grand Canyon without any argument.

When she turns onto the exit for the Grand Canyon, she waits for the questions and the explosion of anger. But there's silence as she heads up Route 64 toward the south rim of the Grand Canyon. She glances back. He's still sleeping. She puts her foot down on the gas pedal and speeds up. She wants to be far enough along that there's no point in turning back.

She's been driving about an hour when Conor wakes up. He knows right away something is not right.

"No! No! This is the wrong way!"

"We're okay! It's okay!"

"Not okay! Not okay!"

"We have to see the Grand Canyon. It's a goodbye to Mom. Remember how much she wanted to go?"

"No!" Conor snaps. "We'll be late."

Mari casts a quick glance to the back seat and sees Conor negotiating with Mom's cell phone, figuring out the time or the quarter of the moon or the declension of the sun or something else he's always talking about.

"It's another four hours and twenty-nine minutes to the highway from there, and we have to go by Route 180. Turn now!"

And then the phone in Conor's hand rings.

Someone's calling Mom. But Mom's not here. Both of them fall silent.

"It's Dennis," he says, looking at the readout on the phone.

"Give it to me." Mari reaches back and feels Conor place the cell in her palm. She pulls over to the side of the road. A huge truck blows by her and rattles the car back and forth, and for a second she's afraid the car will tip over and roll down into a ditch. She looks at the screen. She holds the phone as it rings and rings and rings. Finally it stops.

Why would he call? Mom's gone.

He's not calling Mom.

Dennis is calling Mari.

The phone starts ringing again, and Mari looks at it as if she's holding something contaminated, something that's going to cause a whole lot of trouble unless she washes her hands of it. But it's her mom's phone. It's all she's got left of her, along with the car and the dumb CDs. The phone, in some weird way, seems more personal, more part of who her mom is. Or was.

"This phone is my friggin' life," her mom said once.

Mari lets the ringing wear itself out again. She stares at the phone. It pings and there's a note about two missed phone calls and a voicemail.

Should she listen to the voicemail?

She needs to know what they know. Is someone coming after her? Do they know she has the car? She thinks about getting rid of her mom's cell, but Mari's phone has no time or data on it. They need this phone. It tells them where they're going.

She places it on the passenger seat, looks over her shoulder for traffic, and pulls back out on the road. She'll listen later.

"We're going to miss everything," Conor warns.

"No, we won't."

"Yes, we will."

"No, we won't."

They go back and forth like this until it becomes more hysterical, ridiculous even. Then they're shouting it.

"NO, WE WON'T!"

"YES, WE WILL!"

Finally Mari stops and it gets quiet in the car.

Then Conor mutters it again. "Yes, we will."

"Fine. You're right. We will miss it. We'll miss everything."

"I know," Conor says.

The argument is over.

Chapter FOURTEEN

They stop at a market in the village a mile or so before the gate of the park. Dozens of people—mostly tourists of all shapes and colors and sizes—are going in and out, but no one pays them any attention. Standing at the checkout line, Mari is holding peanut butter crackers and a Mountain Dew. Conor is clutching a huge bottle of bright red soda, which no one should ever put in their body.

Mom would freak out.

Two days ago, buying so much junk food and sugar would have been a sign of rebellion against her mom, but now there's no one to rebel against, no one to make mad. The person behind her is speaking with what sounds to Mari like a French accent, and the person behind him has an accent she can't even identify—he sounds like someone from a spy movie. Nobody cares what she's buying or if the kid next to her is flapping his fingers in front of his face.

Back in the car, they drive toward the park, Mari slugging back her Mountain Dew and Conor drinking his own poisonous concoction. At the entrance gate, they have to wait in line. Mari hadn't even thought about how much it would cost to get into the park. A sign warns them: Thirty dollars.

That's a lot of money.

"It's thirty dollars," the Master of the Obvious calls from the back seat. "We don't have thirty dollars." He climbs into the dog crate, like he's hiding from their lack of funds.

Actually, they do have money, but Conor doesn't know it. He doesn't know his sister rifled through Mom's drawer before they left home.

Mari looks ahead to the person selling the tickets. It's a woman park ranger.

As they inch closer, Mari considers their options. They only have so much cash. If she can get away with charging, it will save money, and she'll never have to pay it back. But charging is a way people can track their movements.

But who would track them? Does anyone care?

She wants someone to care. She wants no one to care.

Mari knows she is going to have to get rid of everything that could trace them. But maybe she could use the card just once more. She's so worried about running out of cash, about having 2,600 miles more to go, she decides to risk it. So she's got the card ready and the window rolled down when they pull up to the booth.

"Hi," Mari blurts out at the woman, putting on a huge grin that catches the ranger off guard. The woman's head moves back in surprise, but then she smiles in spite of herself. "Just a day pass," Mari says, handing over her mom's Visa card. "What should we do if we only have a couple of hours?"

The park ranger, all dressed up in her Smokey the Bear hat and green tucked-in shirt and shorts, takes the card. She holds it out to read it, looks at Mari, then says, "There's a welcome center up ahead—they'll help you there."

Then she sees the dog crate in the back. "You'll have to have a leash for your dog," she says as she swipes the card.

And then Conor barks. Like a dog. One of his only jokes. Except this time he keeps going.

The park ranger leans over and sees that it's a human in the dog crate. She holds the slip for Mari to sign on a little clipboard, her mouth wide open.

Mari smiles and rolls her eyes. "We left our dog at home, but my brother likes it in there. He's a little weird."

Conor is now barking like crazy and the woman gives Mari a rueful grin. The line behind them is backing up, and Mari sees her bluff is going to work. This lady is no cop, and besides, who could get mad at a teenager taking her brother to the Grand Canyon? Mari scribbles on the receipt and hands it back to the woman, who gives her a packet of information.

"Have a nice day," the ranger says. "And your dog, too. Although he really ought to put on a seat belt. Even if he's a dog."

Mari gives the woman her best smile. "Thanks. I'll make sure he does."

They drive off, and as they do, Mari looks in the rearview mirror at the dog crate.

"Nice job, Rover," she says.

Conor barks twice and then goes quiet.

The parking lot is jammed with cars and pickups and huge RVs. Hundreds of people are wandering around or waiting to get into the visitor center. Some are clustered at displays that explain how the Grand Canyon came to be; others are strolling down the paved path to the rim.

"Conor, you have to stay close to me, okay?"

He's walking beside her as they follow the signs to Mather Point, the main destination point for the hordes of tourists.

"I mean it, okay?"

"We can't stay very long," he says.

"I know. We're just going to walk along the path for a little bit. I want to see over the edge."

"We can't stay very long," Conor repeats.

Oh, for God's sake.

We're at one of the wonders of the world and Conor couldn't care less—he's just worried about when we're leaving.

Mari knows that the whole situation with him is very fragile. There are lots of people around, and he's not sure what he and Mari are doing or how long it's going to take. Having him lose it here could be really bad. And sure enough, when she glances over, she sees he's starting to flip his fingers in front of his face again.

Stimming.

It started when he was two.

Conor did it for months before Mari complained.

"Why is he so weird?" she'd finally asked one day.

"Don't ask me," Mom had said. "It's what he does."

Mom was defensive because it drove her crazy too. At first, when Conor started flapping his hands or flipping his fingers, she would grab ahold of them and squeeze, as if that would calm him down.

It didn't. Flapping his fingers and hands and arms was what Conor did to calm himself down. And after a couple of years trying to get him to "friggin' behave," Mom had given up. "This is how Conor copes," she mused one day. "Some people drink beer. Some people smoke a cigarette. Some people hurt other people. Conor flaps his friggin' hands. The world would be a better place if that's what people did when they got upset, instead of hurting themselves or someone else."

Now Mari is prepared when passersby react to Conor's stimming. It happens all the time. Everyone would like to "fix" Conor. Mari would too. She wants him to be able to look at her. She wants to be able to talk with him. She wants the brother that other people have. She wants these things not just for her, but also for Conor. It's painful to watch how hard things are for him. He seems oblivious to how hard it is, but he must know, somehow.

But to some people, "fixing" Conor would mean forcing him to behave so they won't be bothered by his behavior.

Some people would say to put him away, out of sight—in some "Home for Those Who Freak Others Out." Sometimes people who want to fix things don't care if they've solved the problem—they just don't want to see it.

Mari thinks of all this in a flash as she notices a woman walking beside them. When Conor's fingers start flipping faster and faster, the woman looks over and her face darkens. Mari can't help it—she gives her a hard stare. The woman looks away quickly, then casts one more sidelong glance at the both of them. She hurries on down the path, separating herself from Mari and Conor.

Mari's anger and defensiveness rise to the surface, making her feel protective of her brother. So, as they go down to Mather Point, she defiantly walks right beside him so everyone can see that they're together. A skinny dark-haired teenager and a chunky blond kid with herky-jerky motions and strange mutterings. She almost dares people to look at them.

Up ahead, she sees the point they've been heading for, where the earth falls away into openness.

Chapter FIFTEEN

As Mari and Conor walk down the steps, dozens of people mill around—people taking selfies, lined up against the rail posing for someone else, staring out of binoculars, or checking their phones. Mari worms her way through a family of five, the mother yelling, "Logan! Logan! You stay right here! Right here!" She passes a couple of teenagers, a boy and a girl, their arms draped over each other, clinging and fondling in front of the whole human race and the almighty Grand Canyon. She pulls Conor through the crowd toward the railing, hoping he doesn't freak out.

They reach the place called Mather Point, and Mari looks out.

All the yelling and laughing and bustle fades—still there, but receding in her mind—as she looks out at this thing, this canyon.

It is a thing—something itself. But mostly its "thingness" is what's *not* there. A huge empty space opens up before her. About a mile away, the earth rises again, displaying layer upon layer of color—red and brown and dirty yellow and purple. Even purple! Off to the left, making its way through the emptiness, is a winding snake of a path torn by the river. Castles of rock stand like fragile attempts at life, of still, quiet being. It doesn't make much sense to her, how all this could happen, until she realizes that what she's looking at is some deep well of time, visible all in an instant—millions of years expressed in open air and rock. Then down at the very bottom, a bare glimpse of the river that made it. The river is time itself, making time. This canyon is time you can see. She takes in all of this quickly, even though she's surrounded by so many people—a large group of Chinese tourists commandeering twenty feet of railing next to them, a lone man dressed in the latest high-tech hiking gear and peering through pricey binoculars, some people speaking another foreign language, others wearing tons of bling around their necks and wrists. All of them are a blip, a hiccup, here and gone, and she stands there long enough to see them come and go. Mari sees that they're a river too, a human river, leaving their mark in time.

Mom never saw this.

Mari tries to see it for her. Staring out across the enormous gap, she tries to feel her standing close by. Like it should have been.

Conor tugs on her elbow.

"Okay, let's go," he says. "We've spent forty-five minutes here already."

Conor is a river of impatience. He *is* what he wants.

"Let's just walk a little ways," she says.

"No walking! We drive now!" Conor's language has become simple and demanding—another sign that he's getting upset.

But Mari wants to say goodbye to her mom, and she hasn't had the chance. There are too many people here, and Conor is ruining the moment. She turns away from the railing, makes her way up toward the steps that lead to the trail, and doesn't look back. This method is risky, but sometimes it works.

Maybe Conor will follow.

At the top of the steps, where the trail turns to the right along the rim of the canyon, she turns back and sees Conor standing in the middle of the landing, people passing him on either side. He's fidgeting—both hands are twitching, but at his sides. Mari takes twenty more steps, then leans against the railing, pretending not to look at him. He plods up the stairs and heads in her direction. She walks a little farther, like she's leading a stray puppy. Advancing a little at a time, she draws Conor along. He's not looking out at the beauty, which must seem completely pointless to him. The Grand Canyon doesn't concern him, but for some reason the eclipse of the sun does.

They walk in this way, Conor trailing her by forty feet or so, for a good quarter of a mile, and Mari begins to look out at the canyon. The ponderosa pines along the path offer a break from the heat that both radiates down from the sun and rises up out of the canyon. She passes others walking along the path—all kinds, all shapes. Babies and ancients. People who walk, or skip, or can't walk at all—negotiating the path with walkers and motorized carts. It seems like there are more foreigners than there are Americans. The whole world is here.

And then Mari sees a young woman wearing yoga pants and a tank top far off the trail above the canyon. She's sitting at the edge of a point, meditating, or something like it, in front of the whole world.

Mari looks around, wondering where the park rangers are. It seems crazy for people to be out there. But so many people are here, doing so many things, the park rangers probably just give up and talk at the end of their shifts about all the stupid stuff they saw people do that day.

Finally, aware people are looking at her, the woman gives up. With as much dignity as she can muster, she stands and puts her hands together and bows to the canyon like it's some deity. Then she heads back to the path and walks right by Mari, who is still standing there watching her.

Mari doesn't want to meditate. But she does want to be closer to the canyon. For herself, for her mom, for them together. She wants to know this place somehow.

So maybe she's crazy too.

Mari steps off the path and works her way down the slope toward the rock outcropping.

Chapter SIXTEEN

"No!" a voice shouts.

Of course, it's Conor.

It's enough to attract the attention of everyone within earshot.

"I'll be right back," Mari says. "Just stay there."

"No, no, no, no!" Conor squats down on the path and places his hands on his temples, rubbing them vigorously like he's trying to get a genie to come out of his ears.

She wants to get out to that rock on the edge, which she has decided is the right place to say goodbye to Mom.

But Conor won't let her.

It wasn't going to work anyway. The outcropping is too far away.

"Fine," she says, loud enough for him to hear. Then she plops down on a nearby rock. Sitting there for just a minute will have to do. She looks out at the canyon and feels the sun on her body. She crosses her legs, and as she does, her mom's phone slips out of her pocket. She picks it up and holds it in her hand, in front of the emptiness before her, wondering if the phone has her mom's fingerprints on it, or even her smell. Of course not—that's dumb. She wonders if she can listen to her mom's voicemail greeting—*Hi, this is Stef. You know what to do.*

Mari pushes the button to activate the phone and sees an alert about five voicemails.

Damn.

She shouldn't, but she does. She clicks to hear the first message.

> *"Mari, if you have the phone, you gotta call me back. Where the hell are you? What are you thinkin'? I got enough on my plate without you stealing the car and takin' your brother. Call me back."*

And then, the next message:

"Mari, they're gonna figure out where you are. This is the worst thing you could have done. I'm not kidding."

She looks at the phone, then out at the giant open space in front of her. What could Dennis possibly have to say to her? Who is he to her now? Not her dad. Her guardian? No. He doesn't want her. Or Conor, either. And who's going to figure out where she is? She didn't rob a bank. She didn't kill anyone. What has she done wrong, other than being underage and driving?

Okay, and bringing Conor along for the ride.

She looks at the phone again. It's strange—this little device could tell everyone where she is. But it doesn't seem real, compared to the canyon in front of her.

A shadow falls over the screen. Conor is standing behind her.

"What's it say?"

She hands him the phone. "They're trying to find us. Listen yourself."

Conor holds the phone and looks at it, then pushes a key. Instead of putting the phone up to his ear, he stares at the screen like he's listening to a fortune-teller speaking to him face-to-face. So Mari reaches up and pushes the speaker button, then starts the message again. They both listen. Now she can really hear the annoyance bordering on anger in Dennis's voice. He's barely keeping it together.

"They're going to find us," Conor says, "and then we'll be in trouble."

"They don't know where we are," Mari says.

"I don't want to be in trouble. Trouble is bad."

"It's okay," Mari says. Although nothing is okay.

"And they can find us," Conor informs her. "Cell phones send out signals."

"What are we supposed to do?" she asks the Grand Canyon.

Mari holds her hand out for the phone, but Conor doesn't give it back. She sees him staring at it, like there's more it's going to say.

"Give it here," she says, trying to grab it.

But then, suddenly, inexplicably, ridiculously, Conor pulls

his arm back in a chicken-winged windup, then flings the phone out into the abyss.

"No!" Mari screams.

Conor and Mari watch the phone as it soars beyond the lip of the canyon.

"What did you do that for?" she screams at him.

Conor shrugs. "Now they can't follow us."

Mari is panting in frustration.

Perfect.

Mari's forgotten all about trying to say goodbye to her mom. How are they going to get anywhere now? Her anger rises in her, and she's about to let go at Conor, to attack his selfishness and impulsivity. But before she can say anything, the guy she saw at Mather Point appears—the high-tech hiking guy wearing his Lawrence of Arabia baseball cap with the flaps hanging down the back and sides of his head and his jacket with a thousand pockets. His water bottle glints in the sunlight.

"What do you kids think you're doing, throwing stuff into the Grand Canyon?"

Mari opens her mouth. Nothing comes out.

"Are you trying to ruin this place? What if everyone tossed their trash over the side? This is a national park!"

"It wasn't trash," Conor explains, completely oblivious to the man's righteous anger. "It was a cell phone."

Now other people are gathering to see what the fuss is all about.

"Where are your parents?" He looks over at Conor, who is now flapping his hands up and down. "Or are you on some kind of group trip? Where's your leader?"

Mari still can't find any words.

"You two better come with me," he says, reaching out for Conor's arm.

"Don't! No!" Mari pushes the man's hand away. They're nowhere near the edge, but any kind of sudden movement with a three-thousand-foot drop close by is enough to freak out anyone, let alone her brother.

"What are you doing?" the man demands. "You come with me right now!"

Mari looks him in the eye. "Hey, mister," she says in a menacing whisper. "Screw you."

Time to get out of there. It's just way too much to explain.

She takes Conor's hand and leads him back up to the path, back toward their car in the parking lot. Nature Guy follows them from a safe distance.

When Conor and Mari reach the parking lot five minutes later, Mari breaks into a run. Conor runs too. Nature Guy heads toward the visitor's center at a quick clip, probably looking for anyone with the authority to stop these children from their wanton destruction of the earth.

Conor clambers into the back seat and into the crate. As Mari gets into the car, she sees the man walking toward a park ranger near a bus stop. Mari starts the car. As she pulls out of the space, she gets an idea.

This will get him.

She makes a turn down the aisles of cars and drives toward the bus stop. Mari reaches Nature Man before he gets to the ranger. She rolls down the window on the passenger side, looks out the window, and waves. "Bye!" she shouts.

The man's mouth opens in disbelief.

And then they're on the exit road going forty miles an hour, pretty sure that no one will come after them. Who would believe that kids were throwing cell phones into the Grand Canyon?

But Mari is still angry, and now she's angry with Conor. Glaring out at the road in front of her, she says, "Conor, how are we supposed to get to Missouri for the eclipse without the GPS?"

And the Oracle of the Dog Crate answers.

"Route 64 to Route 180 to Route 40 to Route 44."

Right. Of course.

That's why he was staring at Mom's phone so often during the drive.

Who needs a GPS on a phone when your brother has one in his head?

Chapter SEVENTEEN

Mari will remember the next three hours as a brief vacation from the craziness of what is happening. In the middle of the turmoil, she is almost happy. Inexplicably. Undeservedly. Gratefully.

They make a turn onto Route 180 that will take them to Flagstaff. Now that they're on their way and the phone is behind them, she's less worried about being tracked, and she relaxes a little. She's not thinking about what comes next, or if there is a welcome for them anywhere. The sun is shining onto the passenger seat and the windows are open. Somehow, just moving puts her at ease—there is nothing to do but drive. And driving is fun. Steering between the edge of the road and the yellow line is like a laid-back computer game. There's no music on, just the hum of tires and the road ahead, lit by the sun racing away from them to the west. Mari sighs, putting away that nagging question about what awaits her at the end. Driving is a blast, and she's driving away from problems.

And then Conor says, "'Rock Lobster.'"

"What?"

"I want 'Rock Lobster.' It's number four on the yellow one with the red letters."

Mari looks down at the pocket on the door. There are still a couple of CDs she hasn't looked at. She pulls one out and sees it's got a yellow cover with people dressed in some kind of old chic way—very dated. But it has to be the right one. The B-52's. She slides the CD into the player.

"Track four," Conor says, climbing out of the crate and fastening his seat belt.

Mari recognizes it as soon as it comes on—she's heard it before but never paid attention to it or bothered to figure out who it was or what it was about. First there's a driving electric guitar line—kind of goofy, thin and sparse—and the singers spit out the words in a teasing way, like they're pretending to be serious, and knowing they're not. Then these weird voices start squalling, *"Ewwwww!"* The whole song seems like a musical joke—it's just silly. But the beat is undeniable.

Conor chants along in this high wavering voice, *"Rock lobster! Rock lobster!"* bouncing up and down, then mimicking the electric guitar: *"Na na nananana na na."*

"Rock...rock...rock lobster!"

And then Mari's doing it too. The song goes on and on, circling around to the opening guitar line, but faster now, like the band can't contain itself or manage to play the same tempo for that long—a rush to get to the end.

They play the track again and again, Conor bobbing up and down, squealing in a falsetto voice—*"Rock lobster!"*—even when the band isn't singing it. And they're both screeching the guitar lines. *"Na na nananana na na!"*

As they drive through the outskirts of Flagstaff, the open space gives way to buildings and houses, and then, as the song comes to its end for the fourth time, they come to the interstate.

They pull onto the highway and Mari feels like she's home. It's the highway and she knows it's where she belongs. For at least a little while.

An hour later Conor suddenly freaks out. "Pull over! Next exit! Next exit!"

"What? Do you have to pee?"

"No! Exit 233! Meteor!"

"What?" Mari's still not getting it. She hasn't been paying attention to the signs or the scenery—she's concentrating on getting to Missouri. She looks at Conor in the rearview mirror.

"Exit 233. This exit! Meteor Crater Natural Landmark. The crater of the meteorite—300,000 tons. It hit at 26,000 miles an hour. Right here! Look!"

"I thought we were in a hurry," Mari says snidely, but Conor doesn't get the irony. For him, words have one meaning—they're like numbers that mean one thing and nothing else. Otherwise, words are undependable. Like people's faces.

"This is important," Conor explains.

Seeing the Grand Canyon was not essential, but evidently, seeing this meteor crater is.

The exit is right in front of them, and Mari pulls off while Conor spews more information about the crater and tells her to hurry. So they turn onto a side road to see a hole left by something 50,000 years ago.

Mari decides to pay in cash even though it's expensive. She doesn't want to risk the credit card. She wonders how they're ever going to make it—they've only been out two days and have spent a third of their money already.

They join the last tour of the day. The guide takes them out on a walkway toward the crater, along with a dozen other people, and Conor is soon the center of attention. The guide is a preachy woman who lectures like everyone else is kind of an idiot and wouldn't understand the complexities of meteors and heavenly bodies. But despite her haughty efforts, she can't get a word in edgewise, because Conor is a walking encyclopedia. He's delivering information at a million miles an hour, head wagging, arms and fingers flapping. People are looking around to see where his parents are, until they figure out that somehow Mari is his guardian.

Guardian.

The word hits her—she's his guardian.

Not official, but a guardian just the same. She's guarding him from doing something stupid, or from something stupid happening to him.

Conor leads the way around the edge of the crater. The guide is clearly annoyed, since it's HER show and she has funny things to say that always work, but he rarely gives her an opening.

Mari almost enjoys the woman's annoyance. She's happy to let Conor talk nonstop about meteors in general and this meteor in particular. ("Meteor*ite,*" Conor keeps correcting people. "It's a meteorite *after* it lands.") Mari isn't even sure if Conor looks at the immense hole stretching a mile across the desert scrub. He doesn't need to see it—he has it in his mind, along with more than heaven and earth can hold.

Conor is magnificent in his obsession. At the end, two people even thank him, much to the tour guide's further irritation. Conor barely acknowledges their gratitude. He's just doing what he does, saying what everyone should already know.

By the time they climb back into the car, it's six thirty. Mari doesn't know where they're staying the night, but it's not going to get dark for a while. They cruise past Winslow, back out into the desert, as the dry brown landscape gives way to land that's a little greener, a little more forgiving. Hundreds of small evergreen trees dot the landscape, their shadows lengthening. Conor's sleeping in the back.

She pulls off at a rest area when they cross the state line into New Mexico and walks over to a display showing a map and a list of state parks and camping areas. There's one fifty miles away, ten miles off the highway—maybe a place to set up a tent and get away from the hum of the road and the world.

As Mari gets back into the car, she takes a long look at Conor—his face is relaxed, his head resting against the window, his mouth open. She feels an overwhelming sense of caring for him—she's surprised by it—and she thinks again of the word "guardian."

I'm his guardian.

As quietly as possible, she pulls the door closed and starts the motor again, then cruises slowly out of the rest area. No one notices her or cares what she's doing—she is blissfully, safely invisible.

She plays the Gulls again.

Branches like a ladder to the sky
No wings, no way to fly...

Somehow, part of her mom went over the cliff with the cell phone. That was a kind of goodbye she hadn't counted on. Had Mari been so busy trying to keep Conor from doing something stupid that she had taken on her mom's role?

Chapter EIGHTEEN

Her mom didn't always do the right thing.

She'd married Kevin, for one. But maybe Kevin wasn't Kevin when Mom met him. Or not the Kevin he became when Mari knew him.

She thinks of the time Kevin had tried to get Conor to just look him in the eye.

"Look at me, Conor. Look at me!"

"It doesn't work that way!" Mom kept saying louder and louder. "He won't friggin' look at you, Kevin!" She reached over to pull Kevin's arm away.

And then Kevin had freaked out. Like Conor would, shaking

his head and looking down and away. "Don't touch me, okay? Get your hands off me, Stef! I mean it. I just want him to look at me once, so he knows I'm talking to him."

And Mari, standing in the doorway, holding her hands over her ears, had yelled, "He knows! He knows!" She wanted them to stop it because if they didn't stop it, she'd have to go somewhere else and she didn't want to go anywhere else ever again.

It had been hard for her, too, accepting the fact that Conor had retreated inside himself.

When Conor went away...

It was like the beginning of a really bad fairy tale—*Once upon a time, there was a boy named Conor who showed up by surprise, and then one day he went away.*

But the story had really started with Mari.

Mom and Kevin had adopted Mari thinking they'd never have a kid of their own. Mom's friend Julia had a connection with the foster parent organization, so Stef (not "Mom" yet) started checking out the website and talking to people at the agency. Finally she had found Mari. For a while they were a happy family of three.

And then Conor had shown up. A big surprise.

And he was unbelievably cute. He learned to crawl and walk and talk. Maybe he was a little behind some of the other kids his age, but what's normal anyway? Mari loved having a little brother.

And then he got less normal. Sometimes Mari couldn't get him to play with her—he was happier by himself. One day she watched him hold on to a blue plastic building block, rotating it in his hands for almost an hour. She'd tried to get his attention, but he seemed to be in another world.

"Conor won't look at me," Mari had told her mom, and she insisted things were fine. But Kevin grew more frustrated. He held Conor's face in his hands, trying to get him to respond, and Conor just squirmed and looked away.

It got worse. He screamed if you put a shirt on him he didn't like. Confining him to the bedroom for punishment didn't do any good. He was happy by himself. With his block. Or the plastic ankylosaurus. Or the digital watch that he stared at endlessly, watching the numbers change.

Mom put Conor in day care. Everybody needed a break.

But one day, when Mari went with Mom to pick Conor up, the teacher took Mom aside and whispered to her—something wasn't right. Conor wasn't happy there. He got upset easily. He never played with other kids. Mari listened to Mom talk to herself on the way home, denying there was anything wrong, while Conor stared out the window at the trees and street signs, repeating the numbers of anything he saw.

And so, their idea of a "normal" kid disappeared, and Conor became someone else—not what any of them could have imagined. Certainly not what Mari had imagined—she no longer got to be the sister she'd wanted to be. Or Mom, who couldn't hold Conor the way she wanted to. Kevin got more frustrated every day, until he finally yelled, "You can't teach this kid a damn thing!"

Mari wanted to make everything better, but she didn't know how. A couple of times, Mari shook Conor when no one was looking—trying to get through to him in a way the others wouldn't be able to, because she was the big sister. She knew him, and she knew he loved her, or had loved her.

It never worked, shaking him. Mari knew it was wrong

when she did it, and it was never worth it. He would either completely clam up or start screaming. Even thinking of it now made her shiver in disgust at what she'd done.

Kevin seemed to get madder and madder. Like Conor, he retreated into his own world, a world where people had to behave in the way he wanted them to.

So Kevin began to go away too, a little bit at a time.

One day Mari came home from school and found her mom sitting on the front step, smoking a cigarette. Which she never did.

"Your father's gone," Mom had said, blowing smoke out of the side of her mouth, twisting the burning cigarette into the step. "I'm sorry."

And so Mari had tried to forget him.

It's almost dark when Mari exits the highway at the sign for Bluewater Lake State Park. She follows the wandering road through some rolling scrubby landscape to the turnoff for the park. She approaches the entrance carefully, ready to do a U-turn and head out for more driving if she sees someone in a uniform. But there's no one there—it's not even an entrance, really. The pavement gives way to gravel, and then there's a pull-out that looks down onto a lake, its smooth surface barely reflecting the last light the sky holds before it goes completely dark.

She passes a parking area of dirt and gravel, with a little metal box and envelopes to pay for camping, but there's no one there. She spots a dirt road leading down to the lake and, with Conor still sleeping in the back, drives down it until she comes to a rough campsite, a place for a tent defined by creosoted railroad ties. She leaves the headlights on, pulls the tents out of the trunk, and sets them up. She unrolls the sleeping pads and bags, and with minimal complaining on Conor's part, gets him into his sleeping bag in his tent—his private space where he feels safe.

"Where are we?" he mumbles, his hand clutching Mari's arm.

"Bluewater Lake in New Mexico."

"Are we past Albuquerque?"

"No, Albuquerque's tomorrow. An hour or two away."

"It's 987 miles from Albuquerque to St. Clair, Missouri," he says as he crawls into his sleeping bag.

Mari climbs out of Conor's tent, turns off the car headlights, and sits on a railroad tie, looking out on the lake. The crescent moon is in the western sky, chasing the sun, intent on catching up with it in two days. The stars are coming out and the lake is an oval of blackness in front of her. There is not another car in sight. Right behind her, in his little blue pop-up tent, she hears Conor's rhythmic breathing.

"Good when he's asleep," she says out loud, and hears her mom's voice as she says it.

It feels like they're the only two people in the world.

Chapter NINETEEN

Mari awakes to hear Conor outside, then his footsteps as he heads away from the campsite. She pulls herself out of her tent and sees Conor running, legs and arms flailing, toward the lake.

"Conor, no!" she yells.

"Yes!" he hollers back.

"Wait!"

By the time she jogs down the hill, Conor's got his shoes off and is wading into the lake. He stops suddenly, lifts his arms, and screams.

"Gross! It's gross!"

Mari wades in to rescue him. The lake bottom is all silt, and her feet sink into the muck.

"It's gross!" he yells again, frozen to the spot.

He offers his hand and she leads him out of the lake. He stands on the shore, shaking. When she tries to get him to walk up to the tents, he refuses. He doesn't want to walk in his bare feet, but he won't put his socks and shoes on because his feet are dirty. Mari takes off the zippered sweatshirt she slept in and wipes Conor's feet with it, cleaning in between his toes, and puts his shoes back on. And then he's fine.

They climb back up, sit by the tents, and eat some peanut butter on bread. Conor opens up the bag of Edith's chips and they eat all of them. All of them.

Mari isn't worried anymore about proper nutrition. That can wait until they get to Lynn.

If Nana takes them in.

There, looking out on the lake, Mari tries to quiet the anxiety of what's going to happen next and the voice inside her telling her what she "should do" or "has to do."

The sun is shining at a fierce angle, casting clear hard shadows from the scrub brush around them, everything tinged in a golden hue with the newness of the day. Having calmed herself down, she finds a moment of peace.

And then they climb into the car again.

This is who they are and what they do.

"'I Wanna Live on the Moon,'" Conor says.

Mari puts it on. Again.

And then plays it. Again.

And they're off. Again.

The old Honda is using more gas than she thought it would, and every time she puts the nozzle in the car, she feels like she is just draining the money out of her pocket.

A few miles west of Albuquerque, they pull into a service area off the interstate. It's a big station. There are a dozen different islands and so much going on, so many people paying for gas or Cheetos or cigarettes or lottery tickets, she feels, once again, blessedly invisible.

"Let me get the gas first, then we'll pee," Mari says to Conor. "Stay in the car until I come back."

She closes the door and heads toward the station.

And that's when she sees the boy.

She guesses he's tall. Sitting on the curb, smoking a cigarette, he's all legs and knees angling up and down, leaning against a scruffy red backpack.

He looks up at her.

She feels a little jolt inside, in spite of herself. He's striking—his crystal blue eyes leap out of his face, beneath long blond eyelashes. He has a whisper of hair on his chin and on his upper lip, and his hair, a lot of it, dirty blond, is pulled up into a loose, ragged bun on the top of his head. Mari guesses he's seventeen or eighteen.

And then he smiles. Looking at all the miles of road on the backpack and on his ragged green khaki shorts and faded plaid shirt, she is half-expecting worn-down teeth in a crooked, snaggletoothed mess, but they are as white as his eyes are blue—even and straight like kernels on a corncob.

Lying beside his backpack is a cardboard sign with words lettered in black marker. Instead of a city or state, it just says *HOME*.

As Mari walks toward the store to pay, he keeps his eyes on

her, his gaze steady and sure. Mari is aware of it, but doesn't look back. She finally dares to sneak a glance at him just as she's about to pass by, and their eyes meet.

"Hey, California!" he says brightly. Then he leans back and takes a pull off his cigarette out of one side of his mouth and blows the smoke out the other side. He grins.

"What?" Mari says. She glances behind her to see if he's talking to someone else, then back at him. "What do you mean?"

The boy motions toward their Honda. Mari looks over at it. Conor is now walking around the car, flapping his arms.

"License plates," he says.

"Oh yeah, right." Mari can't help smiling back at him.

He grins wider. "You look great when you smile."

Mari shakes her head and feels her face redden. She keeps walking.

Inside, she stands in line to pay and every ten seconds looks back out the door at the boy, who is apparently already thinking about something else. He says hi to a couple of other people going into the store—one an overweight man in baggy shorts and a Hawaiian shirt, and one a mom with a couple of kids.

He's just friendly. He talks like that to everyone.

Mari is a little relieved. And a little disappointed.

She debates whether to chance using the credit card but chooses not to this time. She fumbles in her pocket for the cash and pulls out two twenty-dollar bills. Her throat tightens when she sees how the roll of cash has thinned. The woman behind the counter doesn't even look at her as she takes the money.

"Pump nine," Mari says, handing her the bills.

As she heads back out the door, she decides she's not going to look at the boy on the curb. She hurries to the car, opens the gas tank lid, and unscrews the cap. Conor comes over and stands by her, very still. She squeezes the handle to start the gas, then glances up. Conor is watching something behind her.

When Mari turns around, she sees the boy walking toward them. He's loose-limbed, swaggering as he ambles. He's left his backpack leaning against the ice machine outside the store. He's pulling his hair back up into a bun and wrapping an elastic around it. His arms are tanned and a long line of muscle runs from his hand all the way up to his shoulders.

Her heart skips a beat.

"Hey!" he says, then looks at Conor. "Hey, little man! What's your name? I'm Sky." He sticks out his hand. Conor gives him the once-over, which is what he does to anyone who approaches him unasked. He evaluates the stranger, then looks away.

"He's Conor," Mari says.

Sky, or whatever his name really is, holds his hands up. "No offense intended, Conor. Fist bumps, shoulder shakes, or nods all accepted as a way of greeting." Then he runs through all three options like some kind of hip-hop move, his arms twisting and flexing.

"Sky?" Mari says, squinting at him in the sun. The pump clicks off, but Mari leaves the nozzle in the tank. "That's really your name?"

"My road name—what everyone calls me."

"How come?" Mari puts the nozzle back in the pump. She glances up at him. He's still smiling.

"'Cause of these," he says, pointing at his eyes. "Sky blue, you know?"

"Right." Mari blushes.

"And what do people call you?"

She shrugs. "Mari." She says it the way she wants it to be said, with the softer *ah* sound, and spells it out for him.

"Not Mary? Mari?"

She nods.

"For?"

"What?"

"What are you named for? What's Mari mean?"

Mari shrugs again and her heart beats faster. No one's ever asked her that before. "I don't know," she says, looking at the ground. "It's just my name."

Conor isn't having any of this small talk. He's flapping his hands and looking all around. "I have to pee," he announces, squinting up at the roof of the gas island.

Sky doesn't miss a beat. "By all means, little man. Because when a man has to pee, a man has to pee. Right this way, Conor and Mari, not Mary!" He sweeps his arm toward the store. "The facilities await."

"I've got to move the car," she says.

"It's fine there," Sky pronounces, like he's Master of the Service Station. "There're plenty of pumps. Don't worry."

So they all troop off across the pavement back to the store, leaving the car where it is, filled with gas and ready to go.

Chapter TWENTY

Mari watches as Conor goes into the men's room. She hurries on to the ladies' room. When she comes back, Conor isn't waiting outside the men's door.

Sky is standing nearby, taking in the scene. Everything about him seems relaxed and easygoing. "He's still in there," he says to her.

She nods.

"Where are you heading?" he asks.

"To our grandmother's."

"That's cool. How far?"

Mari doesn't trust people very easily, but she likes it that Sky seems interested in her. His questions seem genuine.

"We have a way to go," she says.

"East or west?"

"East." She tries not to look at his arms. She finds herself wondering what he's doing there and where he's going.

"How far?" Sky asks again.

"A long way." She glances away. For all her bravado and toughness, she's never really had a boyfriend. Her tough exterior keeps people away from her. And anytime a boy seemed interested, her mom watched him like a bird of prey, ready to swoop down.

Conor comes out of the restroom and walks right past them, headed for the snack section. Mari lets him go but keeps an eye on him. Sky is still leaning against the wall, looking nonchalantly up to the ceiling and nodding along to some music that only he can hear.

"Boston," Mari says.

"No shit," Sky says. "You've got to be kidding. Boston? Like Boston, Massachusetts? All that freakin' way?" He is practically bouncing up and down like it's the coolest thing he's ever heard.

"Where are you going?" Mari asks. "Or do you live here in the convenience store?" She dares to tease him, and it works.

They both smile and Sky laughs out loud.

"No, no, no." Sky shakes his head. "You won't believe this, but I'm going to Hartford, Connecticut. At least I hope I am." Then he shrugs and raises his eyebrows like two question marks.

Mari isn't sure where Hartford is, but she knows Connecticut is in the northeast like Massachusetts. Like Nana.

"It's, like, two hours from Boston," Sky explains. "My grandmother lives there and I know she'll take me in—if I can get there."

Mari's breath catches.

His grandmother?

This is all too much of a coincidence, which means it probably isn't true. She realizes he's angling for a ride. But still, Sky doesn't ask the question—either he's too shy or too respectful or too careful. Or he wants *her* to offer.

Mari leaves Sky leaning against the wall to catch up with Conor.

Her brother has found two large bags of Edith's Original Barbecue Potato Chips and has one under each arm.

"No, Conor," she says. "We have to put them back."

"We don't have any more. These are more. We don't know if they'll be anywhere else."

Having paid for the gas with cash, Mari is worried about the money. She's also annoyed that Conor seems happy to push every advantage—she knows that's not what he means to do, but it IS what he's doing.

And then Sky appears at her side, holding up some kind of wallet fashioned completely from silver duct tape. He opens it to show a wad of cash.

"I got this, little man," he says. "Follow me, folks." And without another word, he heads for the checkout line.

So Conor and Mari follow. Sky pays for the potato chips and some gum, and then asks for one of the hot dogs that's been slowly rotating on the hot dog roaster for hours, or days, or weeks.

"Ketchup?" he asks Mari.

"I'm okay," she says, shaking her head.

"Ketchup?" he repeats.

"Um...yeah. Okay." She watches as he squirts a line of red across the top of the hot dog.

He turns to Mari and holds it out close to her face, but not letting go of it.

She takes a bite and realizes how hungry she must be. Even though she doesn't like hot dogs, the taste explodes in her mouth and she is instantly happy—it's delightful. He holds it up for her to take another bite and then he takes a bite himself.

Outside, Conor makes a beeline for the car carrying his giant potato chip bags. But Sky stops at the ice machine where he's left his backpack, and Mari sees a patch sewn on the flap of it. *Why be Normal?* it asks.

Mari stops and looks at Sky.

He smiles. "You're driving all that way by yourself? How many days?"

"I don't know." Mari pauses, then says, "So...thanks." Her thoughts are jumbled. He's going her way. He's probably legally old enough to drive, which is more than she can say for herself.

"I could help with the driving," he offers. "And pay for half the gas."

Mari is trying to be the grown-up. It would be a relief to have someone else to drive, but it feels like there should be a contract—some kind of agreement. "I don't know. We have to stop in Missouri to see the eclipse," she says, halfway hoping this will ruin the whole deal.

"Awesome," Sky says. "Event of the century. The All-American Eclipse!"

Mari has assumed it would be just her and Conor all the way across the country. She hasn't thought about someone else coming on the trip. She doesn't want to explain herself. Or Conor. But she could use some help with the driving. More important, she's running out of money.

Her mom would freak out.

But her mom's not here.

"Okay," Mari says.

"O-KAY!" Sky shouts, skater-dude style. Then, impulsively, he grabs Mari's hand and kneels before her like a knight in shining armor.

Mari laughs. "Jeez. Stop it," she says, blushing.

Sky rises from his knee and slings his backpack over his shoulder. Mari turns to see Conor staring at them, clutching the chips. Before they've reached the car, Conor has opened the back door and climbed across the back seat into the crate and pulled the door shut behind him. Conor doesn't warm to most people very easily, and he certainly hasn't warmed to Sky, chips or no chips.

I need someone to help, Mari thinks. *Conor is just going to have to deal with it.*

Sky stuffs his duct tape wallet into the top flap of his backpack and they cram it into the trunk. They climb into the car and are off onto the interstate.

And so now, Mari thinks, *there are three.*

Two hours later Conor is still in the crate. Sky is driving. He's got a license. "Nothing to worry about," he reassures her.

Sky flips through a bunch of her mom's CDs and pronounces them to be hopelessly lame. Mari nods and shrugs, glad that he didn't put in the B-52's or the Gulls, so she didn't have to lie through her teeth in Conor's presence.

Maybe they are lame, she thinks, seeing them through Sky's eyes.

So instead of playing CDs, Sky turns on the radio and finds a country station, immediately launching into parodies of whatever song comes on, singing in a deep, twangy country singer voice that manages to be simultaneously accurate, on pitch, ridiculous, and beautiful.

He can sing.

The next song is about someone driving down a back road with their eyes closed. Except it's obviously about more than driving. The double meaning hits both of them at the same time. It's not just a ride in a car. Something else is going to happen. Sky stops his chortling vocal, and the chorus comes around again. Mari feels a rush go through her body—it's awkward and uncomfortable and amazing. Her body isn't listening to her head. She sneaks a glance at Sky and he's looking at her with a goofy grin on his face. He shrugs, then looks back out the windshield and drapes his hand over the top of the steering wheel with his bronzed arm stretched out. Mari looks out the windshield too.

And then Sky starts to laugh, and Mari does, too. It's all good. It's just a dumb song. It's not about them.

Twenty minutes later he shifts his left hand to the steering wheel, and his right hand comes out and pats her twice on her knee, then goes back to where it belongs, hanging over the steering wheel.

"This is great," Sky confides. "I'm so glad you picked me up. Thanks."

Her stomach rolls over and her spine tingles. She keeps staring out at the road. She's not sure what to do with all her feelings.

Conor shifts in the dog crate. The Oracle has nothing to say.

Chapter TWENTY-ONE

Over the next couple of hours, as they continue along the highway with Conor asleep in the back, Mari's story comes out. At Sky's prodding, she answers quietly about her mom. And the car. And being a foster kid in the System. And Kevin, and why she's going to Boston. She can feel herself opening up, little by little. It feels scary, but also freeing.

"Didn't your mom and grandmother get along?" Sky asks. "How come she's on the other side of the country?"

"Just where she lives," Mari says. "Where my mom is from."

Mari's not ready to tell him more. Not quite yet. Especially if it makes her look bad, which it does.

Sky doesn't ask about Conor, and Mari is relieved. She can't explain about her brother with him in the back seat. Sky might not understand anyway.

Her mind comes back to Conor again and again, thinking in between the bursts of talk. Does Conor really know he's different? Does he understand? Does he think something is wrong with him? And who's going to take care of him now? What if Nana can't—or won't—take care of him? As Mari thinks about that possibility, her whole body twitches.

"What is it?" Sky asks, his fingers reaching out to touch her shoulder.

"Nothing," she says, flinching away.

Without a word, Sky seems to know whatever Mari is thinking about is forbidden territory, though he keeps casting glances back at the boy in the dog crate.

When they reach Tucumcari, New Mexico, they stop for gas. "You take this one, if it's okay," Sky says. "I'll pay for the next. Promise."

Mari feels a pang of disappointment, and the first real trace of doubt. She dismisses it.

She takes a chance and pays with the card. When the machine accepts it, she's relieved at not having to worry about money for at least another three hundred miles. Sky comes back out of the store with bananas, juice, and potato chips, so she figures he's still planning on doing his part. He opens the trunk and sticks his wallet back in the safety of his backpack. On an impulse, Mari climbs in behind the wheel and holds her hand out for the keys. She wants him to know she still has some control.

"Sure you want to drive?" Sky asks. "I don't mind—"

"For a little while," Mari says.

Sky gives her the keys, then tosses the bag of chips into the back seat.

"These aren't the right kind," Conor says. "I don't want these."

"All they had, little man," Sky says. "Be happy with what you got. That's the secret to a good life."

With that, he elbows Mari in the midriff, giving her a conspiratorial smile, then rolls his eyes.

Mari shrugs, not wanting to acknowledge that she and Sky are somehow united in their disapproval. It bothers her that Sky was setting the two of them apart from Conor. But on the other hand, what Sky said was true, and she was thinking it herself. In a way, she's glad there is someone else there to say it.

"I won't eat them," Conor says. "I know this kind and they're not good."

"We can't go back," Mari says as they pull onto the highway. She tries to find Conor in the rearview mirror. "We'll look next time we stop."

"They were a gift from me, little man," Sky says. "You should take them as a gift."

Conor goes silent again, and Mari can feel herself being put between the two of them.

Stupid boys. That's what her mom would say.

Conor climbs into the crate. "I won't eat them," he mutters.

"Whatever floats your boat, little man," Sky says, shaking his head. He bends down and pulls off his sandals. His seat belt isn't fastened, and he leans his back against the door, swinging his bare feet up on the console, inches away from Mari's arm.

"I'm not a little man," Conor protests. "That's not right."

"Conor," Mari said, trying to soothe him, "just calm down."

Sky rolls his eyes again, smirking in Conor's direction.

Then things get quiet. Mari knows this kind of quiet—the edgy silence that sometimes happens in a warring house. Mari tries to ignore it until finally the tension in the air evaporates, worn away by the hum of the road. She slowly relaxes. She wants to just keep driving. Forever. With the radio off, Sky begins to whistle a tune under his breath. Mari settles back into the seat, letting her shoulder rest against one of Sky's feet.

He grins. It's a killer grin. He presses his foot into her arm.

"I have to pee," Conor says.

"We'll stop in a little ways," Mari says.

"There's a rest stop in seven miles," Conor announces.

Sky shakes his head. "How do you know?"

"I just do," Conor says.

"What? By telepathy? Are you some kind of a genius who

can see into the future?" Sky's tone is sarcastic, and Mari doesn't like it.

Conor doesn't say anything, so Mari does. "Kind of."

Sky chortles. "Yeah, right." He leans in to Mari's shoulder for a brief moment in a teasing bump, and she feels the weight of his body. Then he moves back and the weight is gone, but the impression is still there, her right arm still warm.

Of course, Conor's right. In a few minutes the sign for the rest area and truck stop looms up on the side of the highway. Mari pulls off onto the long entrance ramp toward the gas pumps and the convenience store. They've used half a tank, and Mari plays with the notion of asking Sky to fill it up.

"Maybe we should get gas while we're here," she says.

He shoots a glance at the gas gauge. "Nah. We're good for a couple more hours of driving."

He's right, but Mari's confused. She was hoping he'd be more eager to do his part.

Well, I'm not paying for it the next time, she thinks.

As they troop into the convenience store, Mari's aware that they're a ragamuffin crew, and the addition of Sky makes them look even scruffier. Still, having him along makes her feel a little safer, as if they're some kind of tribe, stronger together. She trails behind Conor as he makes a beeline for the men's room, a single. When she sees he's inside, she hurries into the women's room, hoping to get in and out as quickly as she can. Conor could be in there for five or ten minutes, but could also be out in less than one. Sky shakes his head, realizing he's going to have to wait for Conor so he can pee too.

Mari pees and washes her hands as fast as she can, then rushes out.

Conor's still inside the men's room, and Sky is leaning against the wall, waiting. When he sees Mari, he shoulders himself upright and nods toward the door.

"He's still in there. I keep hearing the water running over and over again."

"He loves the automatic faucets," Mari explains, realizing it won't make any sense to Sky. She knocks on the door. "Conor. Let's go."

The water goes on, then off, then on again.

"So what's with him?" Sky asks.

"He's got autism."

"You mean, like brain damaged or something?"

"Not damaged. Different."

"But weird, right?"

No. No. Please don't. Don't act like this.

"Yeah, I guess he seems a little weird if you don't know him," Mari says, pretending things are okay. "For sure. But it's just who he is. He's okay."

Sky nods, and Mari desperately hopes that's the end of it. The water goes on and off again. Sky pounds on the door. "Yo! Little man. Let's go! People are waiting."

"He's coming," Mari says, her anger rising.

"So, like, you have to take care of him all the time?" Sky asks.

"A little."

"Like, forever?"

"No," she says, trying to smile.

"Wouldn't it be nice if it was just you and me driving around?" He lets his hand rest lightly on her arm.

Part of Mari knows what he's saying, but she won't admit to

herself what it means. "What?" It's all she can manage, but she pulls her arm away.

"I mean, you know, like if there was someplace we could drop him off. If you could leave him with someone, or if he could, like—"

"You mean *dump* him somewhere?" Mari cuts him off, struggling to keep the sharp edge of fury from showing in her voice.

"No, no," Sky says, smiling and shaking his head.

Mari looks into his eyes. She can feel his interest in her— she can almost smell it.

"Not *dump* him exactly. Just find the right place for him, so, you know, it could just be..." He reaches out and encloses her whole hand in his.

The men's room door swings open and Conor bursts out. He sees them standing together, Sky's hand around hers, and his face darkens in anger. He pushes past them, strides down the aisle of potato chips without a glance, and barrels out the door of the shop.

Mari pulls her hand away, but Sky reaches for it again, giving it a little squeeze. "Not like that, Mari. But, like something. You know? We can figure it out, huh? You and me. Let me drain the monster and I'll be right back."

Drain the monster? Give me a break!

He goes into the restroom and she stands there for a moment, stewing. She pounds on the door. "Hey!" she calls to him inside the restroom. "Will you pay to fill up the tank or not?"

"Yeah," he calls back through the door. "Next time, like I said."

Next time. Sure.

Her anger boils over.

I'm an idiot. A complete idiot.

She wants to wrench the door off its hinges and step into the sanctuary of the men's room where Sky is tending to his *monster* and kick his ass from here all the way back to where she picked him up. She wants to scream, *"Who do you think you are, you stupid punk?"* Her whole body is on fire.

If she had a padlock, she'd lock him in. But she doesn't. Instead she turns and heads to the counter. There are a couple of people in line, and she pushes to the front of it.

"Excuse me, sir," she says to the guy behind the counter, an enormous balding man wearing a worn white dress shirt and the look of someone who can't believe he has to do this crummy job. "We gave the man in the bathroom a ride, and we shouldn't have. Before he went into the restroom, I saw him put a bunch of candy bars and stuff in his pants."

Before the clerk can say anything, Mari is out the door. When she gets to the car, Conor is standing there, shaking his head and gazing at his undulating fingers.

Chapter TWENTY-TWO

"Let's go," she says, unlocking the car. "Get in."

Conor doesn't move.

"Come on, hurry!"

Conor looks back to the store, and when he does, so does Mari. The bald man has come out from behind the counter and is confronting Sky.

"Forget him! We've got to go."

And that's enough for Conor. He gets in the back seat, but he doesn't climb into the crate. Instead he just buckles up and huddles down, his hands pressing on the top of his head like he's trying to keep it from flying away. Mari gets the car started, jams it in reverse, and turns the steering wheel. The car lurches backward, spinning three-quarters of a circle before she slams on the brakes, narrowly missing an air pump. As she heads toward the entrance ramp of the interstate, Sky bursts out the door of the store.

"Hey, hey, hey!" he shouts, running toward them.

Mari hits the accelerator and there's a squeal as the tires leave a patch. Who knew an Accord could do that? They hurtle down the quarter-mile access road to the highway, and then she hears Conor say, "What about his backpack?"

His backpack. It's in the trunk. Easy enough to keep going. But then, partly so she can give Sky a last piece of her mind, and partly because she doesn't want anything left of what she's just experienced, she pulls over twenty-five feet from the highway. She pops the trunk and flings open her door. As she steps outside, she can see Sky running for them, waving his arms. He's still a hundred yards away.

When he sees Mari get out of the car, he slows to a trot. "What the hell?" he shouts. "Are you freaking crazy?"

Well, that definitely does it.

She pulls out his pack, undoes the top drawstring, and empties everything out. Then she finds his duct-tape wallet in the pocket on the top flap. She opens it and pulls out two twenties and some fives and singles, then hurls the wallet and whatever's left in it in Sky's direction. When it registers on him what she's doing, he starts running again. She flings the backpack into a ditch, leaving his T-shirts and pants and underwear and mess kit lying on the pavement. She gives them all a kick, then turns back to the open car door.

"Wait, wait!" Sky screams, his voice now more desperate than angry.

"Thanks for the fill-up!"

Mari climbs in, slams the door, and guns the engine. The car hops again, the tires squeal, and she pulls out onto the highway. She doesn't even look back to see the mess she's left, though if she had, she would have seen Sky kneeling in the middle of his scattered possessions.

Her heart is hammering and she's short of breath; the anger in her is fizzing over the top like a shaken soda can, dripping down the sides of her being, and slowly, slowly ebbing. She looks in the rearview mirror at Conor, and sees something she has never seen before. Conor is looking directly at her, and their eyes lock.

And it was Conor who started the staring.

She nods. She has no words.

But he does. "You need to put on your seat belt."

She steers over to the shoulder and buckles her belt. And then they're off again.

Mari turns on the stereo in the car and finds the song she wanted on the Gulls CD. All of the Gulls singing, shouting,

Don't tell me what to do
I don't belong to you
Don't think you know the score
Watch me walk out the door
I don't belong to you
I don't belong to you

An hour or so later Mari is still stewing—she's furious at Sky, or whatever his name is, and she's furious at herself for getting sucked into his crap. And she's even furious at Conor, who

hasn't spoken a word for half an hour. They've crossed over the state line from New Mexico to Texas, an hour or so away from Amarillo, and a feeling has been building up inside her the whole time—she wants something from Conor. She dumped that guy partly for his sake. Conor should know that. He should say something. A simple thank-you. Something.

But he doesn't say a thing.

And he's not going to say anything. She knows this and it makes her madder. Conor wouldn't know what to do with anybody else's feelings even if they were printed out on a spreadsheet in a mathematical equation.

Conor doesn't deal with feelings. He deals with the route they're on, or the need to go to the bathroom or to eat. He speaks up if his shirt is scratchy or he doesn't like the sun on his face. He lets you know he doesn't like it when someone yells— but that's not about feelings, that's about noise. And he hates noise. He can't process it.

It makes her even madder because she knows he can't help it. And it's still not fair.

Not fair.

What in the world *is* fair? Who even came up with the concept of fair? She wishes she never knew about fair, since it's what makes her so angry at the world.

She glances in the back. Conor is looking at his astronomy book.

Perfect.

Astronomy, he can count on—where the stars are going to be in the sky and when the sun is going to rise and set. The moon will pass over the surface of the sun at 1:17 p.m. in St. Clair, Missouri. Those things he understands.

Mari feels like she doesn't understand anything. At this moment she has no idea of who she is or where she's from. She doesn't have a family, other than the kid in the back seat, who doesn't care.

And she's driving all the way across the country to see somebody who probably hates her. Why shouldn't Nana hate her?

"She's a wild thing," Nana had said.

A thing!

And that wasn't fair either. Which is why Mari did what she

did. Which is why they haven't seen Nana for three years. Nana was so hurt at what Mari said and did that she had left them. Without saying goodbye.

Stupid. Stupid. Stupid.

Mari doesn't want to be herself anymore.

On the edge of Amarillo, she pulls off the highway at an exit lined with stores and malls.

"What are we doing?" Conor asks, looking up from the book he is memorizing, alert to the change in speed and the sound of the car tires on the road.

Mari doesn't answer. She'll show him what it's like when someone else won't talk.

She pulls into a shopping area and parks close to a Target. She knows the layout of Target stores—she knows where everything is, and she knows any Target store will have what she's looking for. Mari turns off the motor and listens to the engine ticking from the heat.

After a few moments she gets out of the car.

"Where are you going?" Conor says.

Mari doesn't answer. He can follow her if he wants. She

tries not to care. But when she sees that he's staying, it makes her anxious, which makes her mad again.

In the store, she walks to the left of the checkout lines, down to the main aisle in the middle and halfway across the store, where she turns to the right. She finds what she's looking for—there are three or four different kinds, but she doesn't bother to examine them. She just takes a box and heads for the restrooms at the back of the store. No one notices her. She's walking with a purpose. Grown-ups know where they're going and she does too, and no one bothers her.

She takes the box into the women's restroom. It's empty except for one woman washing her hands. Mari heads into a stall, closes the door behind her, then waits until the woman leaves. She comes out and looks in the mirror. God, she looks like hell. Forget about Conor's wretched appearance—she hasn't changed her own shirt for two days. Her hair is dirty, hanging in hanks, and so is her face. It stares back at her, a tired-looking face, slack-jawed, with pouty fat lips. She hates it.

She opens the box and pulls out electric clippers, plugs them into an outlet to the side of the sink, and stares at herself in the mirror again. Then she goes to work. The hair tangles in the clippers, so she pulls the small pair of thinning scissors from the box and starts to cut. She looks up at the mirror and watches the hair fall to the floor, into the sink, and onto the shoulders of her T-shirt, until it's short enough to shave.

She hears someone coming. She sticks the scissors in her back pocket and turns on the water, pretending to wash her hands. A woman comes in with a little girl.

"Hi," Mari says, hoping friendliness will keep the woman from noticing the hair in the sink and on the floor.

The woman smiles and ushers the girl into a stall, closing the door behind them. Mari decides not to wait any longer. She runs the clippers over her head, going from back to front, then front to back, and the short hair falls off in little cascades. Then she goes back to front again, turning sideways to see if she's getting it all. She hears the mom chatting with the girl over the hum of the clippers.

Mari goes back over her head one more time, trying to smooth out the patchy cut. She's aware, suddenly, of the cool air on her head, on her skin. She peers in the mirror.

"Holy crap," she mutters. She sticks her tongue out. And makes the ugliest face she can.

"Screw you!" she says to the face in the mirror.

The door to the stall opens. In the mirror she sees the mother standing there, staring at Mari holding the clipper, then down at the hair in the sink and on the floor.

Mari turns and faces her. "How do you like it?" she asks, as if to enlist the girl and her mother in her escapade.

"You cut off your hair," says the girl.

"Yep," Mari says.

The mom is quiet, confused. She has her daughter wash her hands and they leave quickly.

Mari drops down on the floor and begins scooping up the hair—her hair, a vital part of who she was, something she used to stare at in the mirror and care about and love and hate—as best she can, then dumping it in the wastebasket. She has to hurry. She turns the water on and wipes out the sink with paper towels. Then, with a wet towel, she begins to mop the floor. She shakes her head at herself—why is she cleaning up?

She puts the clippers and scissors back into the box, places it on the ledge above the sink, and looks in the mirror one last time, seeing a tough, shaven-headed teenager.

"You wild thing!" she says to herself, and leaves the restroom.

Mari walks down the aisle, passes the home appliances and phone accessories and clothing and all that stuff she'll never have, and cruises out the door.

Chapter TWENTY-THREE

Conor hasn't left the car, but he is looking out the window for her. He starts shaking his head when he sees her walking across the parking lot.

"What happened?" he asks when she climbs in and starts the car. As she puts it in gear and heads out of the parking lot, she's surprised at herself. Two days ago she was having major anxiety attacks pulling out of a parking space. Now it's just something she does.

"I cut my hair," Mari says. She glances back at him. He's dropped his head and she sees his right hand begin to twitch, having little conversations, as he adjusts to an abnormal situation. She doesn't offer any more information. At the stoplight near the mall entrance, she turns the rearview mirror to look at herself. In some weird way, she feels free. Or freer than she was twenty minutes ago. Nobody cares what she looks like, and neither does she. She rubs her hand on her head, feeling the short bristles on her palm and fingers. Her neck scratches from the hair that's fallen on it.

They've been on the highway for about ten minutes when Conor asks, "Why did you do that? You don't look like yourself." He's still looking at the floor.

"I don't even know who I am," she says.

There's silence for another five minutes as they're cruising through Amarillo.

"That's dumb," Conor says definitively—a pronouncement and a judgment. "That's dumb to say you don't know who you are."

Mari doesn't say anything, and there's another three or four minutes of silence. Then he speaks again.

"That's dumb," Conor repeats.

"Okay, genius," Mari says, "then who am I?"

"You're my sister," he answers.

Something in Mari lets go. She gives up. She's tired of arguing—with Conor, with the world, with herself. It occurs to Mari that in Conor's mind, her being his sister is another mathematical equation, a fact of physics, like the orbit of the planet Venus or the fact that Amarillo is on Route 40 and 143.7 miles from Tucumcari. Mari is Conor's sister, and a specific number of things follow from that.

Mari thinks about Mom.

Not Stephanie. Stef.

Not an Irish girl from Lynn, Massachusetts.

Mom.

Mari remembers a time when she had done some crummy thing—lost her jacket or punched someone or yelled at some authority figure—she didn't even remember what it was. Her mom was really mad at her and was stacking dishes in the cupboard as loud as she could and Mari was looking for a way to make her mom say what Mari was afraid she would say—that she hated Mari. Part of Mari wanted to prove that things were broken.

Mari had planted herself in the doorway of the kitchen and folded her arms and leaned forward. "Why do you even care about me?" she'd yelled. "Why do you care?"

And Mom had stood there at the sink, her hands resting on its edges, her back to Mari.

And Mari had waited for the explosion.

But her mom had turned and folded her own arms. "I care about you because I care for you," she'd said.

"That's dumb," Mari had shot back, shaking her head. "It's the same thing."

Her mother had let out a deep sigh. "It's like this, Mari. Caring *for* and caring *about* are two different things. You don't care about someone or something or someplace until you care for it. People think it's the other way around. It's not. And now I've been taking care of you for a long time. So I care *about* you and I care *for* you. And I would appreciate it if you'd get that through your stubborn, thickheaded, pain-in-the-ass skull."

Then she'd walked out of the kitchen door to the carport.

It seemed all backwards. You were supposed to care about someone and that's why you took care of them.

"Dumb," she says, to herself, as they pass the last Amarillo exit.

Mari turns the rearview mirror and looks at Conor. Taking care of her brother drives her crazy. Sky (*that asshole!*) was right. It *would* be easier without Conor.

But she has to take care of Conor, and it makes her care about him.

Which is why she'd thrown Sky's stuff out of the car.

"Conor," she says.

He doesn't answer.

"You're right. I'm your sister."

"I know," he says.

After a long stretch of road, passing hundreds of gigantic windmills with clouds towering above them, Mari stops and makes peanut butter sandwiches. They eat them in silence and get back into the car. Mari drives. And drives. The sun goes down, and she drives. Conor announces there are thirty-seven hours until the eclipse. She puts on the Gulls and drives deeper into the night. Listening over and over to the same songs.

"Mom," Mari says softly to herself. "Mom. Mom. Mom."

She'd thought she'd left her behind. There with her cell phone in the Grand Canyon. But she's still here.

Mari drives on.

Chapter TWENTY-FOUR

She missed the turnoff. She realizes it after she's gone through Oklahoma City. It's late in the night and she'd been on automatic, with Conor sleeping in the back. She knows they were supposed to be on Route 44 now, and then she notices the sky ahead of her is growing light.

Conor, her human GPS, is asleep, and she's not sure what to do. Waking him up is the answer, but she knows he'd be crabby, and even crabbier when he found out that they weren't on the right road. She has no map but the one in her brother's head and she's nervous about finding her way.

And they're low on gas.

Crap. Really low.

She slows down to save fuel, but she's pretty sure it won't make much of a difference. She nurses the car along—the gauge flirting with the red, and she's not sure how much money she has left. She used all of Sky's money on the last fill-up.

"Damn, damn, damn," she whispers, pounding the steering wheel. She tries to calm herself—they've done another three hundred miles, and after Oklahoma comes Missouri. But she is exhausted. An electric whining runs through her head and arms and legs.

A billboard beside the highway says, "This is Indian Country—Welcome to the Seminole Nation." At the next exit, Mari spots a sign for an all-night gas station. She pulls off the highway, turns into the station, and eases up to the pumps. She tries to do it as gently as she can, hoping not to wake Conor, hoping she can find out where they are, and hoping to fill up with the credit card just one more time.

She decides to get some coffee.

She doesn't drink coffee. Her mom did. By the gallon. But Mari hated the taste of the stuff—how could something that smelled so good taste so bad? But now she doesn't care what it tastes like. She needs something to keep her going. They were going to have to backtrack or take some side road to get back to the original route, and she doesn't know how long it will take. She wants to fix it before Conor realizes something's wrong.

Coffee first, she thinks. She'll buy the coffee and the gas with the credit card, and then, she promises herself, be done with it. If anyone tried to track them, the trail would run dead in the middle of Oklahoma.

With Conor still asleep, she pulls the card out of her wallet and leaves the car at the pump.

The convenience store is quiet. The sun's coming up and the attendants are sorting out their cash drawers, changing shifts. She goes over to the self-serve coffee station and pulls out the biggest cup there is—it almost takes both of her hands to hold it. Pulling the spigot down, it seems like she's emptying the entire urn into the cup. She stops when it is about two-thirds full, and starts adding one plastic carton of flavored creamer after another—anything to improve the taste of the nasty stuff. It takes a while, and even though the store is practically empty, she feels like people are watching her. She must have emptied ten of those stupid little plastic things, a thimbleful at a time.

Cradling the Styrofoam cup with both hands, she heads for the checkout line. The two attendants are chatting behind the counter. She decides to pay for a specified amount of gas—that way she won't have to come back inside. She girds herself and speaks firmly.

"This coffee, please, and thirty dollars of gas, pump six," she says with a quick, practiced grin.

One of the clerks can't be older than seventeen. The other couldn't be younger than sixty. The older man is wiry, graying hair slicked back, wearing a white shirt with a bolo. His ID tag says *Dale—Assistant Manager*. The two attendants stop and stare at her, and it feels like they are looking right through her. Both look down at the card she holds, then out at her car. Mari looks too. Conor is out of view. Behind her, someone comes up and stands in line, waiting.

The older man takes the card, looks at it, then screws up his lips. "Where you headed, missy?" he asks.

Something in Mari flinches, but she calms herself. "To my grandma's," she says, smiling again.

The teenager has his arms crossed and is leaning back against the far counter, watching the interaction.

The older man nods, then punches in the amount and swipes the card. He waits, drumming his fingers on the counter. Mari has a premonition, a sickening feeling, ahead of his response. She can feel the presence of the person behind her, but doesn't want to look, so she stands there, planted as firmly as she can manage.

"It's denied, missy," the man says. "Want me to try it again?"

Mari shakes her head. Her breaths are coming shorter now. "I've got some money in the car. I'll bring it in if you just okay the sale."

The man is holding the card up in the air, saying without words that he was thinking about keeping it. "Well, missy, why don't you run out there and get me the money, and I'll set the pump for you."

"Okay." Mari holds out her hand for the card, but the man acts like he hasn't seen her do it.

"If you give me the card back, I'll get my wallet," she says.

"What's your name?" the man asks.

"Stephanie," Mari answers evenly. "Stephanie Hammond."

The man frowns, looking down at the card. He's probably

wondering what a girl her age is doing with this credit card. "You go get the money, and we'll see about the card," he says.

Mari feels anger building up in her. Who is this guy to hold on to her mom's card? What does he know? She recognizes he's taking advantage of her and it makes her madder. Because she's a girl. The thought runs through her brain in an instant. Because she's smaller than the men behind the counter. Because he has the power to do it. The anger grows. She knows if it explodes, the trip could stop right here.

She stares at him, trying to calm herself. Dale, the assistant manager, is not used to being stared at by a dirty teenage girl with a shaved head, and he doesn't like it. The younger clerk has a smirk on his face.

She hears the customer behind stepping closer. And then, like some visitation from another planet, an arm reaches past her—a big arm in a Western shirt cuffed at the wrist, holding a card in rough dark fingers bearing several large silver rings with turquoise stones on three of them.

"Put it on mine, Dale," a voice says.

She turns and looks. It's an enormous man. He's dressed in

jeans and worn cowboy boots. His shirt is tucked in, holding in a prodigious stomach that pours over his waist, with a thick belt and silver-and-gold buckle pressing back against the overflow. His hair is silver and gray, thick and long, over his ears, covered by a bent and twisted straw cowboy hat. His face is wide, the color of burnt clay.

He is holding out the card, which is dwarfed by his large, bearlike hands.

And now Dale isn't looking at Mari anymore. His eyes are fixed on the man holding out his card.

Mari has practiced saying no to people her whole life—no to any handouts, no to any kindnesses, for fear of what might follow, what will be expected in return. Afraid of what she'll be asked to do if she accepts it.

But this time Mari says nothing. It is a rope being thrown to her, and she grabs it for all it's worth.

"No need to do that, Michael," Dale says. "She says she's got money. I'll let her go get it."

"No need for her to bother," this angel named Michael answers. "Put it on mine. Along with these Slim Jims and a large coffee."

Dale shakes his head but runs the man's card.

Mari stands still, watching the transaction, dimly aware of all the things that are going on—Dale's frustration, the challenge by Michael, along with his kindness. And she's worried about the card, hoping nothing nasty will follow. She also feels an amazing sense of being protected by someone bigger and wiser and stronger than she is. But even so, she's nervous.

Dale hands Michael's card back to him, with Mari's still in his other hand.

"And, Dale, give her back the card," Michael says softly.

Dale tilts his head. "Now, Michael, it didn't run, and—"

"Just give her back the card," Michael interrupts. "It ain't yours."

For three seconds Mari's whole world seems to hang in the balance—everything could so easily go sideways. Then Dale shakes his head and frowns, handing the card back to Mari.

"Thanks," she says to Dale. And then she looks up at Michael, who is staring at her with an unmistakable kindness in his deep brown eyes. She looks for words, but all she can do is nod—barely even a yes. He touches his fingers to his hat and nods back.

Mari makes her way to the door, knowing all three of them are watching her. Outside, she tries to stay calm, walking at a measured pace back to the car. She pulls open the lid of the gas tank and unscrews the cap, then takes out the nozzle. As she lifts the latch, the machine whirs to life. Inside the car, Conor is still asleep.

As she finishes and replaces the nozzle, Michael comes trundling out of the store, coffee in hand. He opens the driver's door of the pickup parked by the door of the store and starts to climb in.

"Mister," Mari calls. Halfway in the truck, he turns back. "Thanks," she says.

"You take care, Stephanie," he says, and closes the door behind him.

Mari climbs into the driver's seat and leans her head against the steering wheel. In the back, she hears Conor's breathing.

He slept through it all.

Chapter TWENTY-FIVE

"Where are we?"

"In Oklahoma," she answers.

"But where? Are we on Route 44?"

Mari had thought about this. They weren't on the right route, but she was just planning to head north at the next exit, thinking that eventually they'd find their way to Route 44, which would take them to St. Clair, Missouri. She didn't know what they were going to do when they got to St. Clair—pitch a tent on Main Street? Climb on someone's roof?

"We're on Route 40, but—"

"We're not past Oklahoma City yet, are we?" Conor asks. Although Mari doesn't look at him, she can sense that he's beginning to move his head back and forth, as if trying to shake off the wrongness of everything around him. "We're supposed to go on Route 44 in Oklahoma City."

"I know, but we're just going to head north at the next exit."

"Did you miss the turnoff?"

"It's okay."

"What time is it?"

"About seven," Mari says. "We're okay—I'll just turn north at the next exit."

"We have to turn north now!" Conor says in a voice full of furious urgency. "And I'm really hungry. And also, we don't have any glasses. We can't look at the eclipse if we don't have any glasses!"

Mari is exhausted—she's been awake all night and what she really wants to do is find someplace to rest. Her body is completely wired, and all she can think about is the archangel Michael who showed up out of nowhere. If only he could be her dad or uncle or "guardian" or something.

"It's okay, it's okay," she says in as calming a voice as she can muster.

They pull off the highway at the next exit—Okemah—and drive through the town, looking for the main route north. Conor can't help—he doesn't have the route through Okemah memorized, since they were never supposed to be there. So Mari follows a path, not on a map, but in her heart, headed north, with the sun on their right as it begins to climb in the sky. She imagines the moon still below the horizon, setting its course to meet the sun tomorrow, where for just a little while, the sun's brilliance would fall quiet to the moon's presence, and the world would rest.

And then, suddenly, she steps on the brakes, which grind a little, as they have been grinding for the last thousand miles. The car slows. Up ahead of them, she sees a bright yellow water tower with huge block letters on the side.

"Okemah—Home of Woody Guthrie."

Seeing the name of the folk singer makes Mari think of Kevin.

The Kevin who sometimes pulled out his guitar and played that song she liked so much. *This land is your land, this land is my land.*

He'd talked, too, about Woody Guthrie, like he was a myth, a ghost, some kind of god that walked the earth. It was Woody Guthrie who wrote that song "and a thousand others," Kevin had told her. And he knew a lot of them.

"This is where Woody Guthrie is from," she says aloud.

Conor doesn't respond. Woody Guthrie means nothing to him. Mari isn't sure what he means to her, but he does represent something—the best part of who Kevin was, the gift of those songs she still carries. She remembers one called "Deportee," about migrant workers being sent back to Mexico on an airplane that crashed, the one with the Spanish words at the end, saying goodbye.

"*Adios, mis amigos,*" Mari says to herself.

She pulls over to the curb, staring at the water tower.

For thirty seconds she just sits there, acknowledging something—those songs that Kevin gave her, this little trace of goodness in the man who should have been her dad.

Conor starts stimming in the back seat. She likes the quiet and doesn't want anything to interrupt it, so she pulls out again before Conor says anything.

Thirty seconds is what Kevin and Woody Guthrie get.

They zigzag north turn by turn, and in half an hour, they hit Route 44 just outside of Tulsa. Conor calms down. Mari's still exhausted, but after nursing the coffee for twenty miles, she's suddenly wired and feels like jumping up and down.

Omigod, is this what coffee does?

Without thinking about it, she slips in the B-52's CD and soon she and Conor are screaming "Rock Lobster," heading over the Missouri state line.

The finish line is in sight.

Not the real finish line, but the one that will fulfill her promise to Conor. But as soon as that realization comes to light—they're going to make it to the eclipse—Conor begins to obsess about something else.

"We don't have glasses," he says. "We need glasses. The retinas of our eyes will burn if we look directly at the eclipse without glasses."

Suddenly Conor is an encyclopedia of information about eclipse glasses.

"They have to be good ones," he announces. "Some eclipse glasses aren't good and your retinas will burn. They need to be approved."

"We'll find some," Mari says. She's beginning to trust their ability to solve any problem.

"Where?" he says.

And so, with twenty-four hours to go, they start pulling off the road and stopping at any place that might have eclipse glasses—convenience stores, drugstores, supermarkets.

They're all sold out.

This is ground zero of the eclipse, and everybody within the five-hundred-mile belt of the eclipse path has planned ahead for the event.

By the third time they pull off the interstate to look for glasses, the coffee has lost its effect, and now Mari feels a burning in her veins and head. She's beyond tired. Her eyes feel like giant dark holes, and every once in a while they close for a second. Her eyelids droop and her mind wanders. She can't go much farther.

Which is why when she sees the sign for Lake of the Ozarks State Park, she pulls off the highway and heads north.

"Why are we getting off the interstate?" Conor asks, his concern ramping up to a new level. "Where are we going?"

Mari tries to stay cool, even though she's jittery and worn-out.

"We're going to the state park to go swimming and rest awhile," she says. "We've only got a couple more hours to go and the eclipse isn't until tomorrow. I have to rest, Conor. I can't see straight. It's not safe for me to drive anymore."

She waits for an explosion. But when she checks the rearview mirror, she sees he has leaned back in the seat and is gazing peacefully out the window. Just like that. Maybe because it's logical. Who knows?

Five minutes later he speaks again.

"We still need glasses. The right kind."

"I know," Mari answers. "It will be all right."

But now she's the one who's anxious.

Chapter TWENTY-SIX

She pulls into the state park entrance, and after a long drive on the entrance road, they come to a gate. Mari hopes it isn't too expensive—she doesn't know exactly how much money is left in her wallet, and she's afraid to look. Her heart leaps when there's no one at the gate, and she sails through, winding down toward the lake and around it until she comes to a picnic and beach area. Without a word, she parks the car and she and Conor get out. Mari opens the trunk, pulling out sleeping pads and towels. She looks in the shopping bag of food. Nothing left but a little peanut butter, two heels of bread, and half a bag of Edith's Original Barbecue Potato Chips that has somehow mysteriously survived. Conor is cooperative as they tromp down to the beach area and set up in a sunny corner, some distance away from the families and single adults who are lying and baking or splashing in the water.

"I have to rest for a while," she tells Conor.

She's worried about him being unsupervised, but she's too wiped to care. She knows she should care. He's capable of doing something weird—upsetting somebody or running away or something else she can't imagine. But part of her feels they couldn't have made it this far only to have Conor do something that would ruin everything. The universe must want them to see the eclipse.

Conor doesn't say a word. Following their usual ritual, he holds out his hand for the car keys and Mari gives them to him. He puts them in his pocket, takes off his shoes, and runs down to the water, up almost to his waist—his shorts and underwear getting soaked. He doesn't care and neither does Mari.

Conor begins another one of his rituals. He stands there slapping his hands on the surface of the lake, watching the water rise up and fall again, and listening to the sounds of his hands slapping and the water falling back into the lake.

Mari, lying on her back, props up on her elbows. She watches Conor, then watches others as they stop to watch him. A few people look around as if they are wondering who's responsible for him. She doesn't move. He's fine. He'll keep this up for an hour, and if other people have a hard time with it, it's too bad. She lies back on the sleeping pad. The sun is really hot, but she's too tired to care about that, either. She closes her eyes and is gone.

Something wakes her. There's a moment of confusion as she wonders where she is. She opens her eyes to the blue sky, and then she remembers. Their spot is shady. She looks around. The beach is almost deserted now.

Mari has no idea how long she's been asleep. Conor is sitting beside her on his sleeping pad, legs crossed. He puts on a pair of cardboard glasses, then takes them off. He repeats the process over and over again, keeping them off for ten seconds and looking around, then perching them back on his nose.

"Hey," she says.

"These are all right," he announces. He reaches down beside him, picks up another pair of eclipse glasses, and hands them to Mari.

She struggles to sit up. "Where'd you get these?"

"A man," Conor says. "He was from Jefferson City, Missouri, and he gave them to me."

Mari puts them on. Everything goes completely black. She can see absolutely nothing through the lenses. She can't believe the glasses are real and worries that Conor has been fooled, but she's not going to say anything.

"How did he know you needed them?" she asks.

"I told him we didn't have any and we didn't want to burn our retinas and I asked if he had some and he did."

Mari nods.

"I had to ask twenty-one people before someone helped me," Conor said.

Mari is very glad she slept through all of that. She looks around to see if there's any fallout from Conor's interrogations, but the beach is just about empty.

"Where is he?" she says, thinking she should thank him.

"He left after he gave them to me."

"I'll bet he did," Mari says.

"I thanked him," Conor says, adjusting his glasses and looking around. "Three times. I kept going back and thanking him, until he said it was enough."

Mari nods and stretches. She still wants to go back to sleep. She notices the peanut butter jar lying on its side, next to Conor. It is completely scraped clean. The bag holding the bread is empty.

"I ate all the peanut butter," Conor comments. "I was hungry and we didn't have breakfast or lunch."

"Okay," Mari says.

"And the potato chips," he adds.

They find an open campsite. With just under two hours to St. Clair, knowing they will make it, something slows in Mari's mind, and Conor seems strangely calm too.

Mari hopes no one from the state park asks them for a driver's license or any other kind of official papers.

Mari thinks about people asking for papers. All her life, people have asked her or someone caring for her for papers. Half the time, she didn't have the right papers. She sure doesn't have them now. She is without papers. She's adopted, she's too young to drive, she has no license, and she has no parents. The unspoken meaning was that if you weren't official, you weren't really a person.

But Mari isn't seeing it like that now, as she sets up their tents in the early evening. To her, there's the official world and the real world. The official world is papers and people in uniforms and people looking at computer screens to see if they can find her and adults talking over her head.

And then, Mari thinks, there's the real world. It's Conor splashing in the water, singing to the Gulls and the B-52's. It's the unfolding of time spread out over the Grand Canyon and Mom's laugh and Michael the Archangel paying for her gas. And even that jerk Sky, running after them, pleading with them to stop.

The official world wants you to believe it's the real world.

But it's not.

She decides not to worry about getting caught. She's tired of worrying. Mari decides to place her bet with the real world, hoping that it wins, at least for a little while longer.

There's a snack bar a short walk down from their campsite. She counts their money—sixty-four dollars left. She's not sure what will happen when that money's gone. The credit card won't work anymore for whatever reason, and she's afraid to try it again.

Mari isn't sure how they're going to get all the way to Massachusetts on the little money they have left. There must be four more fill-ups of gas to go, which means somewhere around $150.

But they're hungry, and she's tired. So they walk down to the snack bar, where they each get a hamburger. She even orders fries.

They go back to the lake. Conor stands in it again, still in his wet shorts, splashing in his organized, mechanical way. Mari sits on a picnic table, watching as the sky darkens and bats come out, swooping and wheeling above the water, diving and dancing after their invisible prey. When the mosquitoes are too bad to stay outside, they go up to the bathhouse, brush their teeth, and then return to their little campsite.

The last thing Conor does before they call it a day is consult his watch, staring at it keenly for a moment, watching the seconds tick by. His head moves back and forth. He's excited. "Fifteen hours and twenty-seven minutes to total eclipse," he says, his voice calm and deliberate, his mind exploding with the reality of the stars turning above them.

They say good night to each other, climbing into their separate tents, their separate sleeping bags, their separate lives and minds.

In the tent, Mari puts her head on her pillow, but she doesn't go to sleep. Immediately her mind goes somewhere else. Beyond the eclipse. After tomorrow. Because there will be a beyond the eclipse, an after tomorrow, and it's the beyond and after where the real questions are.

And there's Nana—standing silently with a particular look on her face that fills up Mari's whole being and starts her heart banging in her chest. Nana with her face drawn, mouth open, bottom lip quivering, tears in her eyes, and then the lips curling in hurt, then anger. And those terrible words Mari had said to her.

"I don't care if I hurt you. I wanted to hurt you. I hate you."

Oh, Nana. I'm sorry. Please forgive me.

Chapter TWENTY-SEVEN

Mari was eleven then. They hadn't seen Nana since a trip to Boston when Mari was nine. Conor, who was only five, was disoriented in the new place and had clung to Stef most of the time, so Nana had spent hours entertaining Mari. It was during that time that Mari had fallen in love with her adopted grandmother.

Nana read books aloud to her—Mari still remembered scenes from *Pippi Longstocking* and *The Witch of Blackbird Pond*. She took her to the Museum of Science, which fascinated Mari, and to a Red Sox game, which she didn't care so much about, except for that moment when everybody went crazy. The bases were loaded, and when the Red Sox batter hit a home run, everyone stood up and sang *"Bom Bom Bom"* and *"So good! So good! So good!"* Mari had thrilled at the wildness of a bunch of people together experiencing something exciting. Nana took her to a funky little seafood shack where she had insisted that Mari try the whole clams, "with the bellies." When Nana saw the horrified look on Mari's face the moment she bit down on the rubbery clam in her mouth, she'd laughed and told her she wasn't yet a real New Englander. "If you lived here," she'd said, "I could make you into one." Which seemed to mean she wanted Mari to stay.

Mari couldn't stay, but she'd returned to California with a huge stuffed dolphin from the aquarium and a beautiful sweater with silver buttons and reindeer knit into the shoulders.

After that, there were phone calls from time to time—Mari loved spending half an hour talking with Nana about what she was reading, or something good that had happened to her. When Mari got in trouble at school or had an argument with her mom, she could talk to Nana, who always took her side.

And then, three years ago, Nana had announced that she was coming to visit them in Los Angeles. Mari was excited. Her mom had just started a new job at Target, was having difficulty finding childcare for Conor, and was frustrated with Mari's behavior at school. With her mom's temper short, Mari was really looking forward to Nana's arrival. She was eager for an ally—for someone who would stand up for her and tell her she was okay.

But as soon as they met Nana at the airport, Mari knew something wasn't right. Nana was all smiles with Mari, but not with her own daughter. They were polite to each other, but the smiles were icy, and the words were few. If Conor had been there, he would have broken the ice with some endless monologue about dinosaurs or stars, but he was at a sitter's house.

When they got home, Nana stopped just inside the door. Take-out food containers were scattered on the kitchen counter and dishes piled in the sink. A pile of laundry sat by the door, ready to be taken to the laundromat. The mess had never bothered Mari, but now she saw the house through her grandmother's eyes. It was cluttered and chaotic.

Stef offered a quick, defensive apology, but Nana just nodded with pursed lips. An awkward, heavy quiet settled into the house, and Mari felt caught between the two women. She wanted things to be NORMAL, so she ignored the silence and showed Nana where she'd sleep—the pull-out couch in the den. Mari had helped her mom make it up the night before with clean sheets and the blue cotton blanket from the closet. In a true act of kindness, Conor had put a plastic stegosaurus on the pillow to welcome his grandmother.

Nana put her small suitcase on the bed and opened it carefully, as if establishing that there, in that space, things would stay organized. "I have some things for you and Conor," she said.

Mari grinned in relief.

Nana handed her a package that had three things in it. And they were all wrong—a plush toy dragon, a coloring book, and a little bottle of washable fingernail polish. Not even real polish. Gifts for a little girl. Disappointment swept over her. Nana was supposed to be the one who understood her, but these presents showed she didn't know who Mari was anymore.

"What do you say, Mari?" her mom had prompted, and that made things worse. Everyone was treating her like she was a baby. Before she could say something she would really regret, she mumbled a thank-you and sulked off to the room she shared with Conor.

She went to her dresser and pulled out the new black tank top she'd bought with her own money. Even though her mom had forbidden her to wear such a skimpy top, Mari put it on and looked at herself in the mirror. No one who saw her in this outfit would think she was a child. Taking a deep breath, Mari headed back to the kitchen.

Nana and Stef were quiet; they seemed to have reached some sort of truce. But when Mari made her entrance in the skimpy tank top, Nana and her mom both stared at her in shock.

A wave of apprehension passed through Mari, but then she reminded herself that this was what she wanted them to see, to understand. She braced for them to start yelling at her.

But instead Nana turned on Stef. "Is this how you let her dress? Looking like that?"

"It's none of your business, Mom!" Stef shot back. And then she glared at Mari. "Take it off," she ordered.

Mari folded her arms in defiance. "I dress myself!" she shouted. "I have a right to choose what I wear!"

"Mari, you're way too young to wear that kind of thing," Nana said. Then she looked back at Stef, her voice rising. "See, Stephanie? She doesn't listen to you. You're letting her run wild, and you have absolutely no control over her."

"I told you to back off, Mom," Stef said. "Let me handle this." She pointed her finger at Mari. "Take off the shirt."

"No!" Mari shouted, sticking her chin out.

"Take it off!" Stef yelled. "Right now. I mean it, Mari!"

And so Mari did. She pulled it over her head, threw it on the kitchen floor, and stared at her mom.

"Mari, that is no way to behave," Nana said, taking a step forward. "You go in your bedroom and put on a proper shirt."

"Mom! Stay out of this!"

"You need help!" Nana shouted.

Mari was stunned by the two women yelling at each other. She hadn't seen her grandmother act like this before, and even though her mom had yelled at Mari, she felt protective of her, like her mom was the only one allowed to yell at Mari. Her vision was blurring from the rage rising in her. Everyone had lost their minds, including Mari. Without a shirt, Mari didn't know what else to do but escape to her bedroom. As she was leaving the kitchen, she turned to the two women one more time and glared at her grandmother. "I'm too old for coloring books, and I don't need stuffed animals or washable fingernail polish. You can take your dumb gifts back."

Nana's cheeks flushed and her whole body went rigid. As Mari reached her bedroom, she heard her mom say to Nana, "Outside. Not in front of her."

The side door opened and slammed.

Mari put her T-shirt back on and stepped into the hallway. The two women were in the carport, but Mari could hear them trying and failing to control their anger. Spurts of conversation came to her ears.

"Look what living out here has done to you."

"Why do you think I left?"

"She's wild. I warned you it was too much."

"I can handle it! I am handling it."

"No, you're not. You should come back East."

"You're still trying to run my life!"

"You're going to lose her, Stephanie. How's that going to feel? She's too angry! She's too much."

The voices drifted a little way off. Mari went to the front window. The two women were standing at the end of the driveway, arms moving, hands flying, fingers poking at each other. As Mari watched Nana yelling at her mother, the hurt turned to anger again. Mari glanced into the den, where Nana's suitcase was sitting on the sofa bed, open.

The last words Mari heard from the driveway hit her hard. "I promise you, Stef. I know from experience. If you don't start setting limits, she'll just get worse."

At that moment something inside Mari broke. It felt like the only people who had been in her corner had left it.

Now she was alone.

Everything she thought and did followed from that feeling of despair. She was wild and horrible and couldn't be fixed and the only place for someone like that was clear. The System. Right or wrong, the huge flame of hurt blazed before her eyes, and she saw and felt nothing else but that rage.

So Mari went back into the den and pawed through Nana's suitcase, looking for something, anything so she could even the score.

She would show them what wild looked like.

Chapter TWENTY-EIGHT

Somehow Mari has fallen asleep. She wakes up when headlights shine on her tent. She hears an engine idling, and then footsteps, and a flashlight beam sweeps by. She freezes, waiting for someone to call out. After fifteen seconds that seem like forever, she hears the scuffle and crunch of gravel as the footsteps move away. As quietly as possible, tick by tick, she undoes the zipper of the flap of the tent a few inches, and she sees a man standing by her car, writing something on a piece of paper, which he sticks under the windshield wiper. Then he climbs back into his jeep, puts it in gear, and disappears.

She doesn't want to look. She lies awake for half an hour, wondering what to do, and finally falls back asleep.

"We have to go!"

Mari stares at the ceiling of the tent.

"We have to go!" Conor shouts again.

She unzips the flap and pulls it open. Conor is pacing back and forth in front of her tent, flapping his fingers, and even his arms. His tent is already rolled up, along with his sleeping pad and bag.

"We have to go. We have to go," he repeats. A new mantra for the eclipse-obsessed.

"Coming," Mari says. "Give me a minute."

"Now!" Conor says. "Now we go. Now you say yes."

She crawls out of her sleeping bag and steps out of her tent. As she starts to pack everything up, she glances at the car. There's some kind of envelope under the wiper. Apprehensive, nervous, she walks over, barefoot.

Conor is now circling the picnic table, carrying on his conversation with the universe. "We have to go," he repeats.

"The eclipse is at 1:17 in St. Clair, Missouri. We have to go there to see if the sky is clear, and if it isn't, then maybe go someplace else. We have to find a weather forecast. We have to go."

The sun is up and it's already warming the air, but the sky is hazy and grayish.

What a joke. What if we get there on time but can't see the eclipse?

Does Conor get mad at the weather? At God? At her?

She pulls the envelope from under the wiper. She's afraid to open it, but she does. There's a note inside.

> HOPE YOU HAD A GOOD NIGHT'S SLEEP.
> PLEASE SIGN YOUR NAME TO THIS SHEET
> AND PUT $15 IN THE ENVELOPE. DROP
> IT IN THE BOX ON YOUR WAY OUT.
> SAFE TRAVELS. ALL THE WAY FROM
> CALIFORNIA! ENJOY THE ECLIPSE!

Mari feels like Michael the Archangel must have written the note. It's the real world, not the official one. She's received a message from a human, and she didn't even have to talk to anyone.

Conor continues to circle the table, chanting, intoning like a monk casting prayers in all directions. "The eclipse starts at 11:48 a.m. Total eclipse occurs at 1:17 p.m. Total eclipse ends at 1:20 p.m. Eclipse ends at 2:43 p.m."

When everything is packed, he gets into the car without a word, still muttering about the time. He's focused like a professional athlete preparing for a championship game. He doesn't ask about food, so Mari says nothing. They drive through the park, and as they approach the entrance gate, she pulls over and looks down at the brown envelope.

She could just drive through. Even if someone's there, they wouldn't be able to catch her, probably.

Fifteen dollars. Minus the money spent on the meal last night, she's down to fifty-one dollars. And they have more than a thousand miles to go.

She reads the note again. It's too kind to ignore. If the clouds go away and Conor gets to see the eclipse, it will be because this person, this park attendant, wished them good luck. And because he let them sleep. It will be because the universe, with all its wheels turning, saw fit to have this particular person leave the note, and not someone filled with rules and demands.

She reaches into her wallet and finds a ten and a one. Eleven dollars. That will have to do.

Forty dollars, a thousand-something miles, and one eclipse to go.

They stop at a supermarket and buy a loaf of bread and peanut butter. Mari makes herself a sandwich, wondering if she's going to turn into peanut butter. Conor is happy in the back, analyzing and consuming the potato chips they bought yesterday.

On the highway, suddenly Mari's aware that everyone in this part of the state is thinking the same thing. Eclipse! The traffic on the interstate is all flowing with their Honda. There are groups of people in most of the cars—not just single drivers. On the side of an SUV filled with children, she sees a sign scrawled in crayon that says *Eclipse, here we come!* They're all in the stream together, like fish swimming up a river, headed back to where they were born. Or like the whole world traveling to a big block party. Again, she thinks of her visit to see Nana in Boston, of walking along the big street leading to the ballpark. That day everybody was streaming toward the Red Sox game, laughing and anticipating doing something together.

In a rush, like a gentle shower washing over her head to her toes, she feels a surge of joy, like her boundaries are broken and she's part of something else. She feels an excitement about being alive, being here. She didn't even care about the eclipse— it was just something she used to get Conor into the car. But now it's something different and new.

Conor looks up from his astronomy book. "Put on 'I Wanna Live on the Moon,'" he calls. He doesn't notice the stream of humanity all flowing together or see that he's part of it. He's alone.

In a breath, Mari crashes from that joy to a deep sadness— Conor is alone and he doesn't even know it.

Conor is fine alone. And that makes her even sadder—he has barely mentioned Mom. Would he notice if Mari were gone, as long as he had his astronomy book and his Edith's potato chips and got to see the eclipse? Does his world include her at all?

"That's dumb," she remembers him saying. "You're my sister."

Sister. Book. Potato chips. One seventeen p.m., August 21,

2017. St. Clair, Missouri. Sun. Moon. Absence of cloud cover. Path of totality. Eclipse.

It's like a math equation. True. Verifiable.

Is that it? And what if it is? What's wrong with that?

Mari believes he does know. He must need her.

She's his sister.

Another wave passes over her. Her body tingles with what must be love for this boy in the back seat.

Mari puts in the CD and flips ahead. When they get to the chorus, Conor joins in: *"I wanna live on the moon, don't you, don't you?"* He's singing the lead and the answering backup parts, not distinguishing between them at all. Words are words, whoever says them. They're all the same.

"Again," he says. "Play it again."

And she does and he sings it again the same way.

Over and over.

The miles roll beneath their tires, drawing them toward the great big cosmic baseball game at the universal Fenway Park.

That is a metaphor Conor wouldn't care about. Conor doesn't do metaphors. Things are what they are and do not pretend to be something else.

Finally, after seven or eight times of listening to the song, the next song comes on and Conor doesn't object. When the CD starts over again, Conor doesn't notice, so Mari leaves it on, like an old friend. She smiles, thinking this must be what her mom felt, listening to songs that were a million years old, songs that she grew up with. The sadness washes over Mari again, and she goes down, way down, and then she realizes it's the song that's playing—one she hadn't listened to much, but suddenly she hears the words.

> *It's a deep, dark hole*
> *Deep, dark hole*
> *I've got a hurt*
> *Inside my soul*
> *You know I can see through you*
> *And I know that you have one too*
> *We're hurting together*
> *That's what gets me through*

Before she knows it, tears begin to leak out from the corners of her eyes, and snot runs from her nose over her lip, leaving the salty taste on her tongue. She sniffs hard, trying to get it together before Conor sees.

"Why are you crying? What's wrong?"

"Nothing," she says.

"You don't cry over nothing."

"Okay then," she says, sniffing one more time. "Everything."

"How can you cry about everything? Everything includes good things, and you don't cry over good things."

"Just forget it," she says.

"Okay," he says. "I will."

Which is fine with Mari.

Chapter TWENTY-NINE

Before they know it, there's a sign for St. Clair. Now Mari has no idea of what to do. Drive down Main Street in St. Clair, Missouri, looking for the Official Eclipse Viewing Station? Stop at someone's house and ask for directions? Does St. Clair, Missouri, even have a Main Street?

Before she has to decide, the answer presents itself in the form of a highway sign. Two miles ahead there's a rest area.

A couple of minutes later they pull into it and find there are already dozens of cars there. The rest area is in the median between the northbound and southbound lanes, so cars are coming in from both directions. There's a building with restrooms and an information kiosk, and little open-air gazebos with picnic tables. Mari sees a rise of land, a knoll, that is the perfect viewing spot.

She finds a place to park and pulls in. "We're here," she announces.

Almost before she can put the car in park, Conor's out and rushing away in a straight-legged, quickening walk to inspect the rest area, his astronomy book clutched to his chest. He's in such a hurry, he doesn't even ask for the car keys. As Mari gets out, more cars are arriving. It occurs to Mari that this rest area is the place where people will come when they have no other place to go. They don't live in the area, they don't have a place to stay, so they're stopping here. A homeless shelter for eclipse watchers! People are unloading beach chairs and umbrellas and coolers. She's a little nervous about finding a place to sit, so she grabs a blanket out of the trunk and walks up to the rise of land behind the gazebos.

She picks an open spot and spreads their blanket on the grass. Now what?

Just wait and let the sun and moon take care of everything else.

She turns slowly around and around, searching for Conor. Finally she spots him standing in front of a family as they set up their little outpost. His book is under one arm, and with the other he's gesticulating wildly, explaining something. It's about as excited as she's ever seen him. She can hear his voice rise and fall, and she catches a few words now and then. He accentuates certain phrases above his usually monotone voice—"burned retinas" and "next eclipse" and "path of totality." His voice gets more emphatic every time he comes to a number or a date—something fixed and real he can understand.

Mari sits on the blanket and watches, keeping track of Conor as he weaves his way around picnic tables and trees and through the gathering crowd, acting as a tour guide for the eclipse.

Conor was born for this.

Mari watches to see how people react to him. Some are uncomfortable and try to ignore him. Conor seems to sense this, and he moves on to the next person or group. He approaches a bunch of kids sitting on the grass, drinking soda from huge bottles, and stands over them for a good five minutes, lecturing.

She can see they're asking him questions and listening closely to everything he has to say. Suddenly he's the life of the party! He flaps his arms a little as he gets excited, but the kids don't seem to notice.

The hill is filling up. It's like some big outdoor concert or sporting event where everyone is jockeying for a place. And although there's no organization or rules, everyone seems to make room for each other.

People are shielding their eyes and looking up at the sky— it's still overcast and everyone's talking.

"Hope it clears up pretty soon."

"Says here that it might open around noon."

"All we need is twenty minutes of clear sky—that's all we want."

Mari decides not to worry about Conor. She lies back on her blanket, reaches into her pocket for her eclipse glasses, and puts them on. The lenses are completely dark, and the cardboard rims scratch the skin under her eyes and on her nose. She lies back and instinctively turns her face toward the sun in the sky. With the cloud cover, it's a dim, smudgy circle. The temptation to look at the sun without the glasses is really strong, but she imagines that Conor would sense it and disapprove loudly, even if he were five miles away. She leaves the glasses on and stares into the plastic blackness.

She's almost asleep when she hears voices nearby.

"Here?" a woman asks.

"Not enough room. We don't want to crowd anyone," a man answers. When he speaks, she recognizes the Spanish-tinged accent she knows from growing up in LA.

She doesn't want to attract their attention, but she gently pulls the glasses off her face and rolls onto one side. It's a family—a white woman in a yellow sundress, beach bags in each hand. Her shoulders droop from the heavy load, and two kids are hanging on her already engaged arms. The father—brown skin, wraparound sunglasses on a wide face, a cross tattoo on one of his huge arms—has put down a cooler.

Mari looks around her. The man was right. It is crowded. While she had her eyes closed, more and more people spread out blankets and opened lawn chairs. A state policeman is wandering around, which sets Mari on edge until she realizes she's just one more face in a crowd. No one knows she's just driven over a thousand miles without a license.

And here is this family, wondering what to do with themselves. Mari doesn't think. She just speaks.

"You can sit here with us."

"You sure? Your family won't mind?" He looks around in search of Mari's parents.

"It's just me and my brother," Mari says.

Already she's second-guessing herself. *Why did I do this? Why did I offer? What if they don't like Conor? What if he doesn't like them?*

"That's him over there," she says, "talking to those people with the big dog."

The whole family—the mom and dad and three kids—turn and see Conor windmilling his arms, holding his glasses out and demonstrating what they do, why you wear them, what you'll see.

The father nods.

"Are you sure it's okay?" the mom asks.

Even from twenty yards away it's clear that Conor is, well, different. But after they take it all in, they don't seem fazed.

"Sure," Mari says. "It's fine."

"I'm Melody," the mom says. "This is Marco. Our kids, Ariela, Gabby, and Robbie. We're the Cardenals."

"I'm Mari. My brother's name is Conor."

Suddenly, without meaning to be, Mari is part of a bigger group of people and she feels safer. And with that, something shifts.

Melody spreads their own blanket out, overlapping the edges with Mari's. Marco moves the cooler to the edge of the blanket and pulls out a pitcher of lemonade. He gives some to their kids and offers some to Mari. The paper cup of lemonade is cold in her hands, and she takes a sip—the cool, tart sweetness of the drink is a small, unexpected joy.

Gabby, who looks to be about seven years old, reaches into her bright pink backpack and pulls out a baggie filled with plastic beads and elastics. She pours them onto the blanket and asks Mari to help her sort out the colors for a bracelet. Keeping an eye on Conor, Mari helps Gabby choose beads for her bracelet, and then starts one of her own. When she was seven or eight, she would have loved making something like this. Now, twice as old, the seven-year-old part of her takes this activity very seriously.

She fits in. No one would even know she's not in the family—everyone's all mixed up together.

Chapter THIRTY

They ask her where she's from, and she's coy—just saying that she and Conor drove over to see the eclipse and will go back to their grandmother's when it's over (the word "back" being the only outright lie in the sentence).

She's got her head bent over the beads, alternating colors onto the elastic, when a shadow appears. Conor is standing over her.

"What are they doing here?" Conor asks. It's not a question. It's really a statement that says, *They don't belong here.*

Mari's whole body clenches.

Oh no. Please, Conor, please don't mess this up.

Melody doesn't miss a beat. "You must be Conor. Would you like some lemonade?"

"Is it real lemonade?" he asks. "I don't like fake lemonade. They shouldn't call it lemonade if there are no lemons in it."

"Conor," Mari warns, afraid of what comes next.

"I don't like fake lemonade," he says again. "It's not good."

"It's real," Melody says. "I promise." She pours a cup and hands it to him. He looks at it for a good long moment—he's not sure he wants to touch something being held by someone he doesn't know. What if their fingers touch? Conor's hands are at his sides, but they're beginning to open and close. Mari reaches out for the cup, and Melody hands it to her. The three kids are watching, and so is Marco—all around them there is noise and laughter, but it seems far away.

Mari hands the lemonade to Conor, and he peers into it, like he's expecting to see a big turd floating around. His lips purse and he squints. Then he holds the cup to his lips and takes a tiny sip.

"It's good," he pronounces. Then he drains it in three gulps and hands it back to Melody for more. She smiles and fills it up again. He drinks it, then holds the empty cup out to Melody again. "I don't want any more. Thank you."

"Would you like a sandwich?" Melody asks gently. Somehow she knows she needs to approach carefully. "We have egg salad and chicken salad."

"I don't like how mayonnaise feels in my mouth," Conor announces. "It has a slimy texture."

There's another pause. And then something magical happens.

"Well," Marco says, "then maybe you like crunchy. How about some of these?" And he reaches into a canvas bag and pulls out a big bag of potato chips.

Not just any potato chips.

Edith's Original Barbecue Potato Chips.

A family-size bag.

How is this possible?

Conor nods. "Edith's Original Barbecue Potato Chips," he announces. "A 14.75-ounce bag. Family size."

He sits down right beside Marco, folds his legs, and looks up at this stranger, expecting him to open the bag. Marco pulls it open and holds it out. Conor reaches in, pulls out a handful, spreads the potato chips out on the blanket, and begins to arrange them in order of size.

Everyone watches, amazed and silent. No one laughs. No one snorts or looks away. Conor picks up the smallest one, holds it in his hand, turns it around and around on its edge in his fingers, then puts it in his mouth. Smallest first is reverse order, and Mari stifles her surprise.

"Edith's Original Barbecue Potato Chips are the best," Conor announces.

"I think so too," says Marco.

Somehow Melody and Marco know. And so do Ariela and Gabby and Robert. Maybe they know the words "autistic" and "Asperger's" and "spectrum." Maybe they know about the boxes that people are put in. Or maybe they just know that Conor has a way of seeing the world that's different and they don't really care about words or boxes.

And Mari feels even more part of something.

"Home," her mom had once said, "is where you don't have to explain yourself."

No explaining required.

With Conor completely fixated on the biggest bag of potato chips he's ever had, Mari says she has to go to the restroom and will only be gone a minute.

"Go ahead," Melody says. "Take your time."

Mari trusts her, and she's tired—tired of driving, tired of holding everything up, tired of not showing what she feels. She's tired of helping and protecting Conor. And protecting herself. Tired of not trusting anyone.

Standing there, Mari feels a flood of questions wash over her. What does it mean to trust someone? How do you know to trust them? What happens if they do something that hurts that trust? Is everything finished then?

No.

Mom broke her trust more than once. Mom did things that hurt Mari. But Mom stayed. And Mari knows she broke her mom's trust. But she always worked to regain it.

Does trust just happen? Or is it earned? Do you decide to trust someone, or do you just give it instinctively?

Mari doesn't think these questions as much as feel them.

And in only ten minutes she trusts this family. Because she's tired. Because she needs someone she can trust. Because she doesn't know what else to do. Because they've been kind and accepted her and her brother.

And so, with Conor in Edith's Potato Chip Land, Mari gets up. "I'll be right back," she says. "Conor, stay here, okay?"

Conor doesn't answer. Potato Chip Land is more interesting than talking.

"We'll be fine," Marco says. "Don't worry."

"I'll be back, Conor," Mari says again.

"I know," he answers.

Mari heads to the restrooms, working her way through the people. The parking lot is full. There's now a highway patrol car at the entrance. The cop is stopping the cars as they arrive, obviously telling the drivers there are no more spaces.

Everyone who has already found a spot seems happy and excited. There are tall people, skinny people, and bald people, all shapes and sizes. All different colors. Kids with balloons and a guy selling eclipse T-shirts and older people in big floppy hats to protect their spotted, wrinkled skin.

A group of girls about Mari's age stands in a circle, giggling and holding their hands over their mouths—the tall one in the circle is hunching her shoulders so she doesn't look so tall, and another girl keeps pulling her hair back and then shaking it free. As Mari walks by, they all stop and look at her. She has a flash of that old feeling of not fitting in, but she shrugs it off. She knows all of these girls are working hard to fit in—laughing at the right times, wearing the right clothes, resting their hands on their hips just so.

Farther down, Mari spots a group of bikers sitting on their motorcycles. The men are dressed in black leather and cutoff shirts with vests. Several women in black leather pants and big black boots and tats the length of their arms hold cigarettes between their fingers, blowing smoke out the sides of their mouths. Mari observes how similar they are to the teenage girls, only older.

Mari joins the long line to the women's room. The two women ahead of her are talking and laughing, and so are the two behind her—it seems like everyone is there with someone else. The line is slow.

Mari watches the men going in and out of their restroom—not having to wait. One of the women behind her—a bodybuilder type with a fade haircut and taut, tanned arms and legs speaks up. "Look at that," she says. "Maybe we ought to all commandeer those toilets. Just so they know what it feels like to wait."

The women in the line all laugh, and Mari smiles in spite of herself. The woman looks at Mari, grins, and pokes her in the arm. "Ain't that right, honey?"

Mari nods. "Yeah," she says.

"Hey, I like your hair," the bodybuilder says, and her smile shows her full mouth—not a sophisticated, considered smile, just a big old goofy one.

Mari raises her hand to touch her hair, remembers that she has none, and lets out a little laugh. "Thanks," she says.

She's not alone anymore.

Inside the restroom, a dozen women are milling around—waiting for the stalls or the sinks, looking in the mirror, changing babies' diapers, combing their hair. It's like the inner sanctum of some wacky club, and Mari has earned entrance into it. When her time comes, she closes the door behind her and does her business but doesn't get up right away. She just listens to the faucets running on and off, the dryer blowing, and the women talking.

Someone raps on the stall door. "Hey, honey!" It's the woman who wanted to invade the men's room. "I'm gonna pee my pants." There's laughter.

Mari pulls up her pants, flushes, and exits. There's that same big, goofy grin.

"Sorry," Mari says.

"No problem, honey."

Outside, it's still overcast. It's 11:30 a.m. The parking lot is full, and the eclipse starts in less than half an hour.

When Mari gets back to the blanket, Conor isn't there.

Chapter THIRTY-ONE

"He's over there." Marco points to a little dog park. "He's telling people how many minutes until it all begins."

It's hard to believe. Usually suspicious of strangers or outright ignoring them, Conor is suddenly Mayor of the St. Clair Rest Area. Of course, he's not really interacting with people— he's giving out information—but it's totally out of the ordinary for him to behave like this. He's ignoring the noise and chaos and is not freaking out. His focus is laser-like. He KNOWS he knows more about the eclipse than anyone else there.

Gabby has finished Mari's bracelet for her, copying the pattern of colors she started. "Mom tied the knot," the girl says, sliding it over Mari's hand and onto her wrist.

Mari sits on the blanket, keeping an eye on Conor, and does something new—or, at least unusual—herself. She asks Marco and Melody where they're from.

"Frisco, Texas," Melody says. "Outside Dallas."

"Wow! How long was the drive?"

"About ten hours," Marco says. "I drove all night!"

"Big dummy," Melody teased. "I only drove two hours. Big man has to drive."

As the kids roll around on the blanket, laughing, Mari can't help wondering why they couldn't just stay with them. Conor doesn't freak them out, and she would be a good big sister for Gabby.

"Why did you drive all this way?" she asks Marco.

"Because I love the moon," he confesses. "All I ever wanted was to be an astronaut and go to the moon and stand on it and wave back at all the people down here on Earth—kind of nuts, I know. But I ended up a guidance counselor at a high school, which is pretty nuts itself. Kind of like living on the moon, I guess. So this is my astronaut day. The school doesn't even know where I am!"

"Skipping school," Melody says. "Me too."

"What do you do?" Mari asks.

"Seventh-grade English," she says.

And before Mari knows it, she's telling Melody about her favorite teacher, Mr. Gonzalez. She keeps the facts hidden that Mr. Gonzalez is in Los Angeles and her mom is dead and Mari's not sure where she's going, other than a vague idea of her grandmother taking her in. Mari trusts them, but she's not yet ready for *that* kind of trust.

Conor strides up to the edge of the blanket. "THREE MINUTES!" He rotates, addressing the four directions. "Two minutes, fifty-two seconds." He's looking at his watch to make sure he's getting the times right. "Two minutes, thirteen seconds."

Marco leans back on the blanket and closes his eyes. "I'm bushed. Don't let me fall asleep."

No chance of that.

Right at the precise moment, Conor makes his long-awaited announcement: "THE ECLIPSE HAS STARTED."

And with that, Mari and Conor and everyone else lifts their protected eyes to the heavens and looks up at the sun.

There's not much to see. There's high cloud cover and the

sun shines faintly through the haze, but it looks no different from the second before.

"Keep your glasses on," Conor warns.

Mari wants to peek. She's afraid this is going to be one big disappointment, but she desperately hopes that it won't be, for Conor's sake.

Mari takes off her glasses and looks around—everyone's leaning back. Someone at the base of the hill has set up a camera on a tripod and is taking pictures of the sky. Others are just holding their phones up, trying to capture on their little screens what's happening so far above them.

After about ten minutes of staring up, people's interest starts to wane. It's over an hour until the eclipse is total, and looking at the sun through impenetrable dark glasses seems to be losing its magic.

Except for Conor. He's standing in the middle of the blanket with the world buzzing around him, his head lifted to the heavens. He's waiting for a sign.

"Conor," Mari says teasingly, "do you want some potato chips?"

"No," he says.

"Edith's," she tempts.

"No."

He's gone.

Melody gives Mari a chicken salad sandwich and she devours it. And then, for a long time, she lies back, resting her head on her forearms, occasionally putting on her glasses and looking up at the sun to mark the moon's movement across it.

"It's 25 percent covered," Conor says. But this time he doesn't yell. He's announcing it to himself.

A big man dressed in jeans, a faded black T-shirt, and work boots is making his way through the crowd, carrying a cooler. He's headed directly toward them, his eyes fixed on something in the distance. As he reaches their spot, somehow one hand slips off the handle of the cooler, and that end drops to the ground. The top springs open and a lava flow of ice and beer bottles and Coke cans pours all over their blanket, soaking one whole side.

"Goddammit," he mutters. "I'm sorry."

"It's okay," Marco says. And without a word, he and Melody and their kids rise from the blanket and start helping him put things back in his cooler.

Conor doesn't move. He's still staring up at the sky, totally unaware of everyone crawling around him scooping up beer bottles and soda cans and chunks of ice.

"I'm really sorry," the man says again.

"It was an accident," Melody says. "It's just water."

They get everything back in and the guy takes off his baseball cap with *Bardahl* printed on it and wipes his forehead. He's sweating like crazy.

"Thanks," he says. Mari looks at his faded T-shirt. On the front is a Confederate flag and lettering that says *America for Americans.*

Marco smiles, sticks out his hand. "Enjoy the eclipse," he says.

The man shakes Marco's hand, picks up the cooler, and trudges off. Marco and Melody look at each other and smile.

"Fifty percent," Conor announces. "Forty-eight minutes to totality."

Totality. Total. Mari thinks about that. We're in the path of totality. The path of "all."

What is "all" anyway? What is totality?

She tries to think of something that's total.

Looking at the guy in the Bardahl hat setting down his cooler, she thinks about the message on his T-shirt. Mom would have taken one look at it and said, "That guy is a *total* jerk," meaning she didn't like what his T-shirt was saying. Mari doesn't like it either. What's unsaid on the shirt is what matters. To her it means there's no room for people of color, even people like Michael the Archangel, which is really stupid, since his people were here first.

But when Mari thinks back to the guy's embarrassment and his apology, she knows he isn't a total jerk. People aren't total anything. A teacher had once told Mari she was totally useless. Someone had said that Conor was totally crazy, which was so far from the truth as to be ridiculous.

What was total? Nothing.

Except maybe the total eclipse.

But even that was only for a short time, and then it wasn't total anymore, and since the sun and the moon were always moving, they weren't total forever. Nothing is forever. There's no such thing as total darkness.

Nothing is total.

As long as things are moving, they're not totally anything.

They're just alive.

As her mind wanders through all of this, it's getting darker. But not like night. It feels more like the cloud cover is getting heavier. People are beginning to pray to the sky, to the sun, to whatever they could pray to.

"Please open up! Clouds! Please go away."

Some guy down the hill shouts out, "We just want a half hour with no clouds!"

A few people laugh. Then someone starts chanting, "No clouds! No clouds! No clouds!" Soon everyone joins in—the whole rest area chanting as one, like some tribal rite. Chanting for the weather gods to cooperate.

Conor, of course, does not chant. He has his own job to do.

"Twenty-two minutes to totality."

And then, as if the gods or God or the sky itself were listening, the clouds begin to thin. Hundreds of faces wearing goofy glasses pivot up to look at the sun.

"They're going away! They're going away!" someone yells. And the chanting redoubles: "No clouds! No clouds! No clouds!"

It seems to be working.

Mari chants too.

Chapter THIRTY-TWO

Almost everyone at the rest area is on their feet—chanting, clapping, hooting, whistling.

It's just like that baseball game Mari saw in Boston. She remembers that the game had been dragging on forever and she was bored. Then someone got a hit and someone walked and suddenly the whole stadium stood up. Everyone knew something amazing was about to happen. When the next batter hit the ball off the outfield wall, the crowd exploded. Reaching second base, the batter thumped his chest and pointed a finger up at the sky—the sky that held the sun and the moon and all the stars in the universe.

And everyone knows it now.

This is the moment. Bigger than any baseball game, because it includes everyone—this wide swath of humanity in the path of totality and for miles and miles beyond it.

The earth knows it too. As the eclipse gets closer and closer to totality, a wind picks up and blows across the trees, rustling their leaves and sweeping their branches back and forth. Then things begin to fall quiet. People stop yelling and raise their heads, waiting, and so does Mari. A mockingbird calls out from the middle of a nearby tree, cackling, then whistling—the only bird making a sound.

There's an eerie grayness to everything. Mari feels like she's in a movie—everything seems strange and provisional. Temporary. This will only last a short time, but right now it is EVERYTHING—each branch or leaf or person or birdcall is part of it.

Mari puts her glasses back on and looks up. A sliver of sun glows around the edge of the darkness.

"Almost! Almost!" a voice calls out. Someone whistles.

And then the light blinks out as quietly as that. Before there is any other sound, she hears Conor murmur to himself, "Totality."

Just after Conor speaks, everyone starts to yell and cheer. Someone blows on one of those plastic horns they use at soccer games. A person at the top of the hill beats a slow rhythm on a drum. It gets darker. The change is not something she sees, since she's got her eclipse glasses on, but something that she feels. Mari looks down and lifts her glasses for a moment. Everyone is frozen in their places, looking up at the dark hole in the sky.

She wants to hug Conor. She reaches out for his shoulder and touches it with the tips of her fingers. He shrugs them off.

Of course.

Then she feels a hand on her shoulder. She turns to find Melody there in the darkness, surrounded by her family. Gabby hugs her leg, and Ariela holds her hand. Marco is kneeling, his arms wrapped around Robbie. Gabby, still holding on to Melody's hand, reaches out to touch her father's massive forearm.

Mari wishes her mom were here to experience this. To see Conor in all his magnificent quirkiness. To put her arms around both of her kids. And so Mari reaches out once again to Conor and puts her hand gently on his shoulder. When he flinches, she presses a little more firmly, hoping the pressure will calm him, like the security of the dog crate around his being. It works. The two of them are touching, and they're connected to this family that showed up from Texas to share their blanket.

In that moment of touching, a wave of belonging washes over Mari, but it doesn't last. Then comes a wave of *not* belonging, of knowing she is different from them and doesn't belong to them. Her life is somehow broken and she doesn't see how it's possibly ever going to be mended. She knows there's a good chance she's going to show up in Lynn, Massachusetts, and the door is going to be closed to her. Then what will she do?

A sudden and brilliant explosion of light makes Mari jump. Through her dark glasses she sees a small speck of sun, the tiniest sliver, peek out from behind the dark moon. It bursts across the heavens, showering everyone there in its shining. A bright, gleaming light that promises something beyond all promising.

"Omigod," Marco whispers.

Mari feels a giant intake of breath. Everyone—not just this

family, but the entire planet, or at least everyone along the path of totality—gasps. Then she hears a collective sigh, a breathing in and out like one being.

She lowers her head and takes off her glasses. And what she sees around her is as astonishing as what is happening above.

She sees everyone looking up, their mouths open. But she sees beyond that. She sees their pudgy knees and their wheelchairs and their skinniness and their grasping and their wanting and their desperation to fit in. She sees the group of teenage girls peering upward, their neediness and cliquishness forgotten for the moment.

She sees that everyone is broken. Not all broken in the same way, but in myriad, different ways. They may try to hide it, but they are.

Mari is broken too. She has lost her mom. She gets mad too easily. She has a bad mouth. Some people look at her funny because she's a foster kid or because she's adopted or just because she is who she is.

She's not alone. It's the hiding of the brokenness that keeps everyone alone.

She belongs to all of this. It's being broken that makes her part of it. Part of being alive.

People laugh and hug one another, disregarding differences and seeing sameness. Birds start calling like it's morning. A breeze riffles across the grass and through the crowd.

Conor stands there, staring at the vanishing eclipse.

Mari puts her glasses on again and watches the sun come back. The moon passes on by, inching ahead of her brighter sibling.

"Goodbye," Mari whispers to herself.

Fifteen minutes later, people are starting to leave. They've seen what they came to see, and it's time to go home.

"A little while longer, then we have to go," Marco says. "Back to school for us."

Conor doesn't move. He's still standing there in his special glasses, head lifted, tracking the movement of the sun and the moon. Mari's torn. She wants to stay here, where she feels like she and Conor are accepted. But now that the eclipse is winding down, there's somewhere else to go.

Her neck is aching from looking up. She takes off her glasses and sits on the blanket, still damp from the *America for Americans* guy's spilled cooler. She sneaks looks at Marco and Melody.

Marco is folding lawn chairs and piling stuff on top of the cooler.

"Do you have far to drive?" Melody asks her.

Now. Now you say yes. *"Yes. It's too far to drive. And I don't know if we'll have a home, because our father left and our mom died, and I don't know if our grandmother will take us in, and I'm only fifteen so I'm not even supposed to drive. Can we come with you? We promise not to be a bother. I'll take care of Conor. He's really smart. Could you? Please?"*

"Not too far," Mari answers.

Melody looks at her and frowns. "Is there anything we can do for you?"

"No, we're fine," Mari says. "Conor wants to stay and watch the whole thing. We'll leave when he's ready."

Melody reaches into the cooler and pulls out four or five sandwiches. She places them in a bread bag. "Here's some food for the trip."

"It's okay," Mari says. "We don't—"

"It's okay for you to take them," Melody says. "Please do."

Mari takes the bag. "Thank you."

"Do you have enough gas to get home?" Marco asks. There's a deeper, broader, more dangerous question lurking there. But he does not ask it out loud.

Please ask me.

"I think so," Mari says.

Marco screws up his lips and gazes at her. He reaches into his back pocket for his wallet, pulls out two twenty-dollar bills, and hands them to Mari.

"No, I can't," Mari says.

"Yes, you can." Marco stuffs the twenties into the bag of sandwiches Mari's holding.

"I'll pay you back," Mari pledges, her voice quavering.

"Pay it forward," Marco says. "Give it to someone who needs it."

Mari smiles and nods.

Gabby wraps herself around Mari's waist for a good long second.

"Goodbye, Conor," Melody calls as they head down the rise to their car.

Conor stares at the sky.

"Don't go," Mari whispers to herself. "Don't go."

But they do.

Chapter THIRTY-THREE

As soon as the Cardenals are out of sight, Mari is ready to get back on the road. She just wants to get to Boston. She wants to find out what's going to happen to her and Conor.

On the way to Boston

On the way to Lynn

"Time to leave, Conor," she says. "We have a long way to go." He doesn't respond, but when she gently pushes him off the blanket so she can fold it up, he doesn't complain. He's still in communion with the heavens. He's not ready to go. Not yet.

So she sets up the expectation like her mother always did. "We're leaving in five minutes."

"There's still forty-five minutes of the eclipse left."

The clouds are covering the sun again, but Conor doesn't care.

"We'll watch the rest of it from the car. You can sit by the window and see it."

He doesn't say anything. So she waits a little longer.

"Three minutes," she says. Then she announces two minutes, then one.

So when she says it's time, Conor removes his glasses and sprints to the parking lot. As soon as he gets into the car, he puts his glasses back on, turning in his seat to face the sun again. Mari dumps the still-damp blanket and the bag of food in the trunk and climbs in behind the wheel. She backs out and exits the rest area, heading toward the highway.

Into the biggest traffic jam she's ever seen. Even bigger than an LA freeway traffic jam.

An hour later the traffic is still just inching along. Luckily, Conor is asleep, but Mari can't help growing more agitated—

she wants to keep moving. They're still twenty miles from St. Louis. Gas is running low again.

"I want to go home," Conor says from the back seat. Evidently, he's awake now.

"We still have a thousand miles to go to Nana's," Mari says.

"No. I mean *home*."

Mari is so flummoxed, she says nothing.

"To Los Angeles. To home," Conor says.

"We can't go home," Mari says. "Mom's not there."

"It's still our home and I want to go back. Dennis will take care of us."

Dennis? How crazy is that? Dennis never wants to see them again. Then Mari realizes that Conor doesn't know what she overheard Dennis say in the hospital—that she's a pain in the ass and Conor's "not right" and "crazy." She has protected Conor from all that.

"Dennis can't take care of us. We have to go to Nana's."

"Dennis knows us better. We haven't seen Nana for three years. She's old. Mom's mad at her. I think Nana doesn't like us."

An arrow goes through Mari's heart. Conor might not know what happened three years ago, but he can see the result. He can see that they're not connected to their grandmother.

"We have to go to Nana's," Mari repeats. "It's our only option."

"No, no, no, no, no," Conor says.

Mari shoots a look in the rearview mirror and sees Conor putting his hands over his ears. His head starts wagging back and forth. "Don't say our only option. Don't say that. Now we go home. Now we go home."

Even though they're barely moving, Mari pulls the car over onto the shoulder. They're between exits, and on either side of the highway are dense woods. Cars creep by them. Mari turns around in her seat and faces her brother.

"Conor, please. Listen to me. Now *you* say yes. It's why we've come. We have to go to Nana's. We can't go back to Los Angeles. There's no one there to take care of us."

"Dennis will take care of us."

"No, he won't."

"Yes, he will. Yes. Dennis will take care of us. We can live in our house. Dennis will live with us!"

How did Dennis become the savior all of a sudden? Since when has Conor liked Dennis?

"No, he won't!" Mari says, anger and frustration climbing up inside her.

"Yes, he will! Yes, he will! Dennis! Dennis! Dennis!"

"He won't! He doesn't even like us!"

"Yes, he does! He likes me! Dennis likes me!"

And before she can stop them, her words pour out.

"No, he doesn't! I heard him say he wouldn't take care of us! He hates us. He called you crazy! He said something's wrong with you! He called me a pain in the ass. He doesn't want us! That's why we had to leave—so we don't get sent to some crappy foster home where no one loves us at all. We have to go see if Nana can still love us. Dennis hates us!"

Conor never stares at anyone, but now he is looking straight at Mari. His eyes are twitching back and forth. This is going to be a really bad one. He unbuckles his belt.

"Conor, I'm sorry. It's the truth."

Before she realizes what is happening, he opens the door and flings himself out of the car and stumbles across the shoulder, down into the ditch that lines the highway and up the other side.

"Conor! No! Stop!"

There's no stopping him. He vanishes into the woods. In the middle of Missouri. A thousand miles from anywhere like home.

"Shit! Shit! Shit! Shit!" she yells to herself. She is so enraged, she can't see straight. She unbuckles her belt and shoves the door open—so hard, it bounces closed again. She kicks at it— if she could, she would rip it off its hinges. She jerks it open, reaches inside for the keys, and cuts off the motor. Furious and terrified, she tumbles into the ditch and scampers up the other side, hurling herself toward the woods.

"Conor! Conor! Wait! Conor! Please!"

She runs without direction for a minute or so, then stops, gasping for breath, her heart slamming against her chest. She's surrounded by trees and dense undergrowth, the sound of the highway behind her. Mosquitoes swarm around her, landing on her arms and legs and neck.

"Conor! Conor!" she calls, panting, stumbling ahead, unsure of where she is going, hoping when the time comes, she can find the car again by following the highway noise. As she catches her breath, she tries to order her thoughts.

I'll keep looking until I find him. I can't leave until I've got him with me.

All she wants is Conor back. The only thing in the world.

"I want Conor!" she wails. Then she wipes the snot off her face and dries her tears and keeps walking, back and forth, back and forth, combing the woods, calling out Conor's name again and again.

Chapter THIRTY-FOUR

Ten minutes later she sees some motion through the low branches of the trees, almost at ground level, then spots a patch of light blue. It's Conor's T-shirt. He's sitting cross-legged on the ground beneath a scrub oak, rocking, swatting methodically at the mosquitoes that are happy to have found him.

Mari is afraid if she says the wrong thing, she'll lose him again. She'll never get him back in the car. Suddenly, she has an insight. She thinks about the times she's flown into a rage, and asks herself how she would want to be approached. How does she want someone to talk to her after she's exploded?

And so, she does that with Conor.

She works her way quietly through the trees, approaching

him as she would an animal in the wild—not wanting to scare him away. A step at a time. Finally she's standing in front of him. Wiping tears from her eyes, she carefully sits down beside him and doesn't speak. If Conor notices her, he doesn't say so. He rocks forward and back, still swatting at mosquitoes. Mari and Conor sit like that for a few minutes—although it seems like an hour. Mari bites her tongue, waiting for him to speak first.

Finally, after forever, he does.

"It's wrong."

Mari doesn't say anything.

"This is wrong."

Another long silence.

"What's wrong?" she asks.

"I don't know. Something. Dennis says I'm crazy."

"You're not crazy."

"Cletis said I'm a freak."

"Who's Cletis?"

"He's a man at my school," Conor said. "He sweeps the cafeteria with a big broom."

"Cletis is wrong."

"Then why did he say that? What's wrong with me?"

Mari's heart opens. He's never said anything or done anything to show he knows he's different. Mom explained to him that he's different, but it never seemed to get through. Up until now he just seemed to accept everyone as part of Conor's World.

Surely, Conor has heard cruel words like these before—Mari knows he has. But here, finally, he's standing outside himself, looking at who he is. The pieces don't fit and he wants to know why.

"What is it?" he asks.

"You're just different," Mari says. It's a crummy answer, but it's the best she can give. "Your brain is different from other people's brains."

"Other people don't have good brains," Conor says, his eyebrows furrowing.

Mari shoots out a short burst of a laugh.

"It's not funny that someone doesn't have a good brain."

"I know," Mari says.

"Some people make a lot of mistakes. They forget where things are or don't know numbers or don't follow directions. Their brains are bad."

Mari nods.

"What is my brain?" he asks. "Their brains are bad. What is mine?"

She thinks for a moment, and then says, "Beautiful."

Conor shakes his head. "A brain isn't beautiful. It's not pretty. It's wrinkled and would be bloody if you opened up your head to look at it."

"Right," says Mari, and she smiles. "But your brain works beautifully. It works differently. So some people think that's wrong. Or weird."

The mosquitoes are biting, but they both just keep swatting them away. The wind blows through the trees and a drizzle of rain starts to fall. Mari hears the drops striking the leaves.

"What's wrong with you?" Conor asks.

"What?"

"There's something wrong with you. You get angry. And you fought with Mom. And Dennis called you a pain in the ass."

"I am a pain in the ass," Mari says.

"That's dumb," Conor says. "You're not a pain in the ass. You're a female human. So you're either a woman or a girl, but you're still a girl because you're not all grown up."

It was beginning to rain harder.

"Conor, we have to go to Nana's. If we go back to Los Angeles, they might put us in a foster home. And that would be horrible. And they probably wouldn't put us together. We have to stay together no matter what. That's why we left when Mom died."

"You're adopted," Conor said. "Mom adopted you."

"I know." Mari sighed.

"So, you're my sister."

"So, you're my brother."

It was pouring now. Their heads and arms and shoulders were soaked. The trees were bending under the weight of the rain.

"Why is Nana in Boston? Why doesn't she ever visit us? Why is Mom mad at her?"

Through the open window of the den, Mari could hear Mom and Nana arguing—not all their words, but their voices, rising and falling, piercing the air and her heart. The two women closest to her in the world didn't seem to care that they were standing out where everyone in the neighborhood could see and hear how horrible Mari was. She heard Nana saying that word again: "wild."

Pawing through her grandmother's bag, Mari found a little velvet jewelry bag, pulled it out, and held it up—it was maroon with emerald green trimming, a gold braided drawstring pulled tight and looped once in an overhand knot. Mari fumbled open the knot and poured the contents onto the bed. There, lying faceup on the bedspread, was the opal, shimmering with a life of its own, embedded in its delicate gold setting.

The voices sounded even louder than before. Mari couldn't feel anything but the brooch, now hidden by the clenching of her fist. She couldn't see anything but what was at the center of her gaze, the ivory opal burning in its own universe. Then, as if stepping into a dark tunnel, she walked out of the den and into the kitchen. She opened the junk drawer and found the hammer. The next thing she knew, her knees were scraping on the concrete floor of the carport and the hammer was coming down and down again. A scream came out from somewhere inside her as the opal cracked, then broke into pieces with each hammer blow. The gold lacing was smashed flat, then torn apart.

Mari sensed the two women standing over her, screaming at her. Stef pulled the hammer from her hands. Nana's screams turned to sobs. Mari watched as her grandmother sat down on the milk crate by the kitchen door, rocking back and forth and whimpering.

Still full of anger, Mari couldn't stop herself. "You're not my grandmother!" she shouted. "You're not my nana! I don't care if I hurt you. I wanted to hurt you. You called me wild. I hate you."

And then Mari ran down the driveway, down the middle of the street, with Stef screaming at her to stop. Mari looked back once at her mother standing in the street, torn between

Mari and her own mother. Then Mari turned and ran again, lungs burning, tears hot on her cheeks. She slowed to a walk and kept going, block after block, through neighborhoods and down streets of taquerias and laundromats and McDonald's and shoe stores and tuxedo rentals. When it was getting dark, she thought she heard her mother call, as if in a dream. But it WAS her mother, driving the car alongside her, with Conor in the back seat. Mari got into the car, but by the time they got home, Nana was gone.

Mari waited for her mother to bring it up, but she didn't—it just sat there, unspoken, for days, then weeks. Finally the entire episode seemed to be forgotten or gone and there was some sense of things being normal. But it was a new normal, since Nana wasn't in their lives anymore.

And it was her fault.

"Everything was my fault."

"What do you mean your fault?"

"I broke something of hers. And she got mad."

"What did you break?"

"A piece of jewelry."

"How did you break it?"

"With a hammer."

Conor paused for a minute. This was something to consider.

"Were you trying to fix it?"

"No, I was trying to break it."

Again, Conor pauses, thinking.

"That was dumb."

"I know."

"Is that all? You broke something?"

Mari exhales. "No. I told her I hated her."

Conor's head shakes. "Why?"

"I don't know. I was mad. And that's why she's mad at me. And that's why we haven't seen her."

"Do you think she's still mad?"

"I don't know."

"Maybe she got it fixed," Conor said. "If it's fixed, then she shouldn't be mad anymore."

"I don't think anyone could fix it," Mari says. She winces,

thinking about the brooch smashed and broken on the carport floor.

"Maybe you could get her a new one. Then she shouldn't be mad."

"Maybe." Mari stands up. "We should get back to the car."

With no argument, Conor follows her.

The rain has stopped. The sun has come out and is shining through the trees, the leaves glistening. Mari listens for the sound of traffic and hears it off to the left, so they wander through the trees and bushes until they come out of the woods with their Honda directly in front of them.

And leaning into their car from the passenger side is a state trooper.

Chapter THIRTY-FIVE

He's going through the glove compartment. The back passenger door is open too, and it appears that the cop has examined the whole car. His cruiser is parked behind theirs, with the lights flashing. As he pulls himself out of their car, he sees Mari and Conor, who are frozen in their spots on the other side of the ditch, about fifty feet away. Mari can't decide if she should turn and run. She takes Conor's hand and he doesn't resist.

"Hey," the cop calls. "Is this your car?"

"Uh-huh," Mari answers.

"Come over here, will ya? What've you been doing?"

Conor's hand in hers, she leads him down into the ditch and up the other side, stopping in front of the trooper. He's tall, trim, and closely shaven, his eyes a fierce gray. He's wearing his Smokey the Bear hat. His leather belt and holster and big boots are shiny and stiff. The gun in the holster is as menacing as anything she's ever seen.

"What are you kids doing here?" he asks.

"My brother had to go to the bathroom and couldn't wait," Mari says.

"Actually, I ran away," Conor adds helpfully.

The trooper grimaces and shakes his head. Traffic is still just inching by, and Mari can hear the trooper's radio calling out for him.

"Where are your parents?"

"It's just us," Mari says.

The trooper shakes his head again, a troubled look spreading across his face. "Can I see your license?"

Mari looks away, then up at the trooper, then over at Conor, who is staring back toward the woods.

"I don't have it," she says.

"What?" The trooper plants his fists on his hips.

"She doesn't have a license," Conor says.

"Where is it?" the trooper asks, closing his eyes in disbelief. Mari sees a trickle of sweat glisten on his neck, then trickle down into his shirt. The radio in his car squawks louder and he gives it an exasperated look.

"I lost it," Mari says quickly before Conor can speak again.

"The plates here say California. Did you drive from California without your license?"

Mari nods.

"How old are you?"

"We're driving to our grandmother's," Mari offers.

The radio squawks again. The trooper glances over, then looks back again at Mari.

"Your grandmother?" His mouth twists to one side. "Where does she live?"

"Boston," Conor says, still looking away.

Mari notices that one of his hands is beginning to flap. He has barely recovered from the world's biggest meltdown, and Mari isn't sure what it would take to trigger a relapse.

"Boston, Massachusetts?" The cop is incredulous.

"Actually, Lynn, Massachusetts, which is eleven miles north

of Boston." Conor speaks in that flat, matter-of-fact tone that can be so infuriating to someone like this cop, who wants Conor to realize that he's in trouble.

"Look at me, son," the trooper says. "Are you okay?"

Conor, of course, won't look at him. The man's face has too many signals in it, and Conor could never make sense of them all. Algebra or trigonometry or calculus are easier for him to understand than a mad cop's face.

Conor's refusal to look doesn't help.

"Are you okay?" the cop asks again.

Conor shakes his head no.

The radio squawks again. "Six-five-three. Six-five-three. Accident at mile thirty-nine. Do you copy?"

"Okay, you guys, you're going to have to get in my car. Let's go."

Mari doesn't budge. Neither does Conor, whose arms are starting to flap more insistently.

"It's okay, Conor," Mari says.

"Let's go, son," the trooper says. "Let's all get in my car." He reaches for Conor.

"No! Don't!" Mari screeches. "Don't touch him!"

The cop stares at Mari in surprise for a moment, then grabs Conor's upper arm and begins to pull.

And Conor freaks.

Spectacularly.

Stupendously.

Magnificently.

He lets out a high-pitched squeal and doubles over. The trooper tries to keep ahold of him, but Conor is like a bronco out of the chute—writhing and twisting, his back, arms, legs, neck, and head all going in different directions, and the pitch of his scream is higher than anything Mari's ever heard.

"Aieeeee! Aieeeeeee!"

The cop lets him go and takes a step back.

But being released doesn't calm Conor down. It's too late. He buckles over, still standing, but with his knees bent. He bows down at the waist so his chest is touching his thighs, his arms out flat to the sides like the wings of a plummeting jet. His neck is taut and his face is turning red. Wagging his head back and forth, he emits short bursts of screams.

"What on earth is wrong with him?" the cop asks.

"He has autism!" Mari shouts over the screams.

"Is he crazy?" the cop asks.

"He can't stand it when people touch him," Mari says. "I just need to get him to our grandma's."

Suddenly Conor stands up straight and launches himself into the back seat of their car. In a flash, he has rocketed into the dog crate and pulled the door shut from the inside. He begins to bark. Then growl.

The trooper puffs up his cheeks and blows out air. His radio crackles. "Six-five-three. Six-five-three. Do you copy? Roland, where the hell are you? There's a three-car at mile thirty-nine westbound, EMT on the way. What are you doing?"

Mari takes a deep breath. She's not sure what to do, so she'll just have to wait and see what comes next.

The trooper makes a decision. He raises his index finger and points at her. "Okay, listen to me. You stay right here. Do you understand me? Stay right *here*. I'm going to answer this call, and I don't want you to move." He starts backing away. "You stay there until I come back. All right? I'll be back soon. Just stay right there."

Mari nods. Conor is growling in the crate.

The cop strides to his car, gets in, readjusts his hat. As his car passes, he looks at Mari and shakes his head. The traffic makes room for him and he does a U-turn across the median onto the other side of the highway. With his siren blaring, he disappears from view.

Mari has a flash of insight. She's not sure if it's right, but it's such a bolt of clarity, she doesn't question it. When the trooper shook his head at her, he didn't mean no. He meant just the opposite. He doesn't want them there when he gets back.

Who would?

She jumps into the car and turns the key. The motor roars to life, but she sits there. She's not sure what to do, how to get out of the traffic.

"I don't think we can stay on the interstate," she says out loud.

The Oracle of the Dog Crate speaks. "Get off at the next exit. Route 141. South to Route 30 to Route 255 to Interstate 55 to Interstate 70."

"What?"

Conor repeats the route.

"I heard you, but how do you know? We don't have a GPS anymore."

"The map at the rest area," he says.

The car idles on the shoulder while Mari looks for a place to get into the line of traffic.

"There are too many cars. You have to drive on the shoulder."

And so she does. For the next six miles, with the cars to the left of her stuck in the post-eclipse traffic jam, dozens of them honking at her all the way for breaking the rules.

If they only knew.

Chapter THIRTY-SIX

Following Conor's directions, they get off the interstate and onto a country road without incident, and in an hour, they're driving alongside the Mississippi River. She had heard about the river in stories and songs. Now here it is, wide and rushing and real.

The interstate bends to the right and carries them over the broad, churning band of water. Off to the left, she sees a gleaming arc of metal stretching into the sky. It changes in shape and feeling as the car moves forward. She risks a look back. The empty space beneath the arch is an openness toward something—a space you should definitely walk or drive or sail through. There's no time to stop and examine it, though somehow the image of it stays with her. She's passing through a mystical opening with her adopted brother and her mom's rattling car and all the baggage of her life in tow.

On the other side of the river, Mari lets out a sigh. She feels a little safer, like she's left the cops behind. She knows the trooper saw the California plates, but hopes he didn't have time to write down the license plate number. She dares a smile, knowing she kept her promise to Conor—she got him to the eclipse. She told Conor the miserable truth about Dennis, and she survived the biggest breakdown Conor has had in years. Maybe now they're heading for a new and better place.

Then she glances down at the gas gauge. The needle is sliding below the half-tank mark. She starts worrying again. They'll never make it.

After another hour and a half of driving, she pulls off for gas— the gauge isn't quite down to the red yet, but she's not really sure how much fuel is left. They pull off the highway and into a Phillips 66 station. The moment she stops at a pump, Conor wakes up and asks for the keys and some money. She gives him the keys, then reaches into her wallet and hands over three dollars. She knows she should save every penny for gas, but just the fact that he's not stimming and seems focused are enough to make her relent.

Sitting in the car, Mari pulls the rest of the money out of her wallet and counts it. Eighty-seven dollars. She holds the bills in her hands and tries to calculate how far they still have to go and how much gas and food this will buy. They're probably looking at around a thousand miles. She guesses they can average twenty-five miles a gallon. She finds a pencil in her backpack and scratches the numbers on an old receipt. A thousand divided by twenty-five. Forty gallons. Gas here is $2.67 cents a gallon. She needs at least a hundred dollars. And that's without food.

Before she can pump the gas, Conor is back with two small bags of cheese curls. Evidently, cheese curls will do if Edith's Original Barbecue Potato Chips aren't available.

"Any change left?" she asks.

Conor gives her seventeen cents.

Mari goes in and gives the attendant twenty-five dollars, which won't quite fill the tank. She has sixty-two dollars left.

"I'm still hungry," Conor says as they pull back onto the road. "I don't want peanut butter."

Mari doesn't answer. Conor crawls into the crate and doesn't say anything more. She wonders how long the peace and quiet will last.

And so Mari drives. At this point, driving is more of a feeling than an action. She puts on the Gulls and listens two or three times in a row to the songs that somehow track her experience. As it grows dark, and the road before her stretches out straight and even, with the *bump-bump, bump-bump* of the pavement on the tires, Mari sings along softly as the singer talks about burying someone, and how she knows someone else is hurting, how everyone has their hurts that they hide. About living on the moon.

And a song about looking at photographs.

There's just one guitar, strumming every once in a while—an electric guitar with a shimmery feel that echoes across the song. The singer's now-familiar voice breaks as it sings about the photograph taped beneath the rearview mirror, so she is looking at two things in the past—the road behind her and her memory of the time she shared with the person in the picture.

A picture of her mom appears to her—she sees her mother's face on the windshield.

Her mom.

Mari wonders how a song that isn't about you becomes about you—how it becomes more than what the singer intended. And then she sings,

What if it was just us two?
You and me, me and you
Side by side
Turning round the sun?

Mari sees Conor and herself as the two moons, or planets, spinning around the face of their mother, and she feels her heart break open a little in some gratitude or contentment or even joy, which is ridiculous. The absurdity of her feeling happy and contented makes her smile to herself, and she gives thanks for the sun and the moon that met today and the hum of the tires and her brother in the back and the road ahead. She would be happy to go on like this forever.

On the last song, the band is roaring, and the singer, this person Mari feels like she knows, is talking about what she's putting in her car—her *amps and axes, boots and belts.* She says she has to leave to find her way, and then she breaks into the chorus.

It's not too late to change your mind

Leave all of this hurt behind

Not too late to change your heart

Even as things fall apart

Come along with me

Come along with me

Mari looks in the rearview mirror and sees Conor, head leaned against the door, sleeping. She breathes out a long sigh. Then she glances down at the gas gauge again. It's below the quarter mark, and the anxiety comes rushing back.

She tries to settle her mind, but it insists on running around in circles about everything that is or could be wrong. When she sees a sign for a gas station, she pulls off the interstate. The gas station is closed. Disappointment, frustration, and exhaustion hit her all at once. But there's nothing to do but get back onto the highway.

Fifteen miles down the road, she spots a gas station lit up at the top of an exit ramp and gasps in relief. Conor's asleep. She drives into the station, gives the attendant twenty-five dollars, and pumps the gas. She shouldn't spend any more money, but she remembers the buzz she got from the coffee earlier on. Will it work again? She hopes so.

As she hands over two singles, the attendant—a young woman, her body pouring out of a tight pink V-neck T-shirt, her hair streaked with bright green and purple—leans over the counter and says, "One of your headlights ain't right, honey. Better get that fixed. You don't wanna get pulled over."

Mari turns and sees that only one of the lights, which she'd left on, is working.

"Yeah, thanks," she says, then trudges out of the shop. She sits in the car, sipping the hot coffee, thinking over what to do.

Thirty-five dollars left. And seventeen cents. One more full tank of gas, maybe a little more. She goes back to the trunk and looks in the cooler—there's an empty peanut butter jar, a plastic bag containing a heel of bread, and a bruised apple floating in the melted ice. The sandwiches Melody gave them are long gone. If she drives with one light out, they might get pulled over and they won't be able to run.

Conor throwing a tantrum saved them once, but it is not a strategy.

Her strategy is to drive and hope.

The coffee works. Mari drives around Columbus, Ohio, then north and around Cleveland. The sky begins to lighten on the horizon. The gas gauge inches down as they leave Ohio behind and come into Pennsylvania. She sees a sign for a state park, and knows she should stop there for some rest.

She stops for gas, splurges on breakfast sandwiches, and drives on to Erie Bluffs State Park. Mari falls asleep by a boat ramp, while Conor stands in the water, splashing. After an hour nap and a quick trip to the restrooms, they pile back into the car.

They head out of Pennsylvania toward New York.

Thirteen dollars left, a broken headlight, no food, and at least five hundred miles to go. She doesn't know how they'll get there, but part of her simply can't believe that the universe would deny them at this point—surely they've been through enough.

When Conor says he's hungry again, Mari tells him they have to save the rest of their money for gas.

"But I'm really hungry," Conor repeats.

"So am I," Mari says.

"I'm hungrier," Conor says. "I'm the hungriest."

How do you measure someone else's hunger...or loss...or happiness?

"Okay. You're the hungriest of everyone," Mari agrees.

"Hungriest of everyone," Conor says to himself. "Hungriest of everyone, hungriest of everyone," he repeats over and over. "Hungriest of everyone."

In a little over two hours they come to Buffalo, New York.

There, without warning, Mari is confronted with a tollbooth.

A tollbooth?

They don't have money for tolls.

She spots a lane for cars that have electronic passes, so she drives through it. She braces for the sound of a siren, sure that a state police car will come after them. Heart jumping, breath short, she looks in the rearview mirror—sometimes it seems to her that she's been looking in the rearview mirror her whole life, waiting to be caught for who she is.

Mari decides that who she is, right now, is just fine.

Maybe the universe thinks so too, because no one comes after her.

Late in the afternoon the gas gauge drops below the quarter-tank mark. The New York State Thruway seems to go on forever. Mari nurses the car into a service area and puts ten dollars' worth of gas in the car. Gas on the toll road is really expensive, and it barely buys three gallons. She gives Conor the keys to hold and two dollars and lets him go into the food court. He comes back out with two hamburgers.

"How did you do that?" she asks, amazed.

"I told the woman this is all the money I had, and she said that was exactly how much it costs."

Mari shakes her head and smiles. Either the woman was kind, or she was freaked out by this odd kid.

They've got a little more than a buck left and half a tank of gas.

Chapter THIRTY-SEVEN

It begins to get dark.

Conor asks for "I Wanna Live on the Moon" again. And again.

They pass signs for Syracuse and keep going.

There's less than a quarter of a tank left. She sees a sign for a service area. How far will a dollar get her? The next area is thirty-five miles away, but she decides to risk it, wondering what happens if you run out of gas on the New York State Thruway. Probably the cops would come and ask for her license and run a check on the car and take her away somewhere. And Conor would have to go live somewhere else—not with her—

to some other universe, some other moon and sun far away from whatever galaxy the official world decides to put her in.

She knows she's coming to the end of something—to the end of the way things were.

Mari notices a sign on the highway—"Albany 84, Boston 250."

They are one tank of gas away from their grandmother and the gas gauge is on red. The Gulls sing about the road and the river. With the orange light on the dashboard flashing on and off, she limps onto the ramp, coasts into the Indian Castle Service Area, and stops at the pump. She's got one dollar—she can't go in and ask for a dollar's worth of gas. They would laugh at her. That would barely be one third of a gallon—maybe good for ten miles.

Mari turns off the engine and looks around. No one else is there. She doesn't see anyone in the kiosk by the pumps. Then she notices that the food court and restrooms are under construction and closed. The only way to buy gas is with a credit card.

Conor has to pee and asks for the keys. Mari starts to tell him the restrooms are closed, but then sees that they've set up portable toilets under the streetlights on the service area pavement. She hands him the keys and watches him hurry across, walking straight-legged and purposefully, jingling the keys in his hand.

Not knowing what else to do, she gets out her mom's credit card and tries it.

Denied.

She's standing by the Honda, lost, when she hears the roar of a motor coming off the ramp. A huge motorcycle pulls in behind her. The guy riding on it is as wide as the bike itself. In his black leather and Darth Vader–like black helmet, he looks mythic, like a character from some dystopian novel or video game. He cuts the engine and pulls off his helmet. There's a rim of white beard around the lower edges of his face, and a do-rag over the top of his head covers the rest of his hair. He stretches and groans and pulls on a chain attached to his belt loops. A big wallet emerges from his back pocket, and he unzips it to pull out a credit card.

Before she can think about what she's doing, Mari walks up to him.

"Excuse me, sir," she says as he starts to insert the card into the pump.

He turns and looks at her.

"I need some help," she says, trying to keep her voice strong. "I'm about to run out of gas. I don't have any money. My mom's credit card won't work. I need to get to my grandmother's house in Boston. I just need one tank of gas. One fill-up. Can you help?"

It's more help than she's ever asked for before. She feels exposed and vulnerable.

The man frowns. His forehead wrinkles. Deep lines run from his strong, broad nose, angling toward the edges of his mouth. He looks like the biggest, oldest, wisest man on earth. Someone from *The Hunger Games* or *The Lord of the Rings*.

"You in trouble?" he asks, looking her right in the eye.

Mari blows out a little breath. Then she forces a smile, gambling that a little teasing might not hurt. "Only if I don't get a tank of gas. My grandma's waiting on us. I'm sure she's worried."

Maybe that's not true. Maybe no one is waiting on them. Maybe no one cares they exist.

"Who's us?" the man's low voice crackles and purrs.

"Me and my brother. He's in the porta potty," Mari says, gesturing toward the line of portable toilets.

The biker looks across the pavement to where she's pointing. There is no sign of any other human. There are only two people on the planet—this girl and this man holding a credit card, who could be the answer to her prayers. He looks back at Mari, weighing her story, her appearance. His hand is still holding the credit card, hovering over the slot on the pump.

Mari stands still, not breathing, and their eyes meet for a good, long moment.

The biker gives a small nod, walks over to Mari's pump, and inserts the card. He punches the buttons, pulls out the nozzle, and holds it out for her to take. Her heart beating like crazy, tears filling her eyes, she takes the nozzle from his leather-gloved hand. She fumbles with the gas cap, sticks the nozzle in the tank, and presses the handle. Mari watches the numbers rise on the display, not once daring to look at the man, afraid she might break a spell that seems to have encompassed the whole night. The pump bumps to a halt. She puts the nozzle back, screws on the cap, and closes the lid.

Now she looks over at him, her gaze even and steady. "Thanks. Thanks a lot."

The man shrugs. "Everybody needs a little help," he says. "No use in not lending a hand. You sure there isn't anything else?"

She shakes her head. "No. We'll be fine."

"Okay. Good luck," he rumbles. Then, as if he senses she would not, could not, say anything more without unburdening everything she is feeling, he puts the card in the slot and turns to his own business, filling the tank of a motorcycle half the size of Mari's mom's car.

Mari walks away from the car and stops about ten feet from the toilets to wait for Conor. She turns to see the stranger put his helmet back on and start the engine. Impulsively, she takes two steps forward as he pulls out. She waves and waves. He lifts his hand in salute and moves on into the night, his engine rising and falling as he goes through the gears.

The world opens to her. She could spread her arms and hold all of it.

The cosmos is generous.

People are kind!

She's lucky!

For a moment Mari is quite sure that Nana will take them in and things will work out. They have to. Conor was right. Nana has even forgotten about the brooch. Everything will be fine.

Conor is still in the porta potty.

"Conor," she calls. "Let's go."

There is no answer.

"Conor! Let's go! We've got gas! We can make it!"

It's silent. Still excited that they will finish their journey, Mari walks along, examining the toilets. The first three are empty—a green circle on the handles shows they're available. She pulls open the doors, one after the other, and finds no one. The last one, to the far right, is closed. On the handle is a red semicircle showing the word OCCUPIED.

She taps lightly on the door. "Conor, let's go. We've got gas."

It's quiet, but then she hears feet shuffling on the plastic floor of the cubicle.

She knocks harder. "Conor, come on! It's time to go!"

Nothing.

But finally she detects movement and pictures him standing in the darkness of the toilet, rocking back and forth.

"Are you all right? Does your stomach hurt?"

"No."

"Open the door then. We have to go."

"No!" he says again, more forcefully.

"What do you mean?"

"Don't come in," he says.

"Conor, what's wrong? We have to go."

"We can't. We have to stay."

"Conor, open up, right now!" She sounds like their mom, and the commanding tone works. The handle moves and the circle turns to *VACANT*. She pulls the door open.

Conor is standing there facing a side wall, his head moving back and forth, his arms flapping at his sides.

"What is it?" Mari asks. "Did you get sick?"

He wags his head back and forth, four, five, six times, arms flapping like a baby bird with no idea how flying works.

"What's wrong? Did you throw up or something?"

"They fell," he says.

"What?"

"They fell. I didn't mean to, but they fell. It's dark." Then he turns and looks down into the open seat of the toilet.

And Mari understands.

Chapter THIRTY-EIGHT

"They fell. They were jingling and my zipper stuck and I was going to wet my pants and they fell."

Mari steps up into the porta potty, pushes Conor aside, and looks down. The smell of everything—urine, crap, chemicals, toilet paper—rises up to meet her, but there in the night, all she sees is darkness. The keys could not be farther away or more invisible if they had fallen into a black hole at the edge of the universe.

"Shit!" she yells. "You dropped the keys into the toilet? How could you do that?"

Conor rushes out of the porta potty and hops around the parking lot in circles, holding his hands to the sides of his head, rubbing his temples. He turns to her, bends over at his waist, and then straightens up.

"They fell! They fell! They fell! I couldn't help it! They fell!"

"No! No! No! No!" Mari yells, which only makes Conor rub his head even more fiercely. He is emitting little yelps and gasps, hopping around like a demented rabbit. "They fell, they fell!" he screams.

"No! No! No! No!" Mari shrieks.

She raises her head and looks up into the black night—the overhead lights of the service area are hiding the stars and universe beyond. She looks down and sees her small shadow falling around her on the pavement. Mari drops to her knees and holds her head in her hand. Soon she's wagging it back and forth, harder and harder, and it begins to take her out of her body, away from what just happened. For a moment she's like Conor—she sees it clearly—she's no different. Conor is blaming the keys and she's blaming Conor and there's absolutely no difference, because neither of them has any control over the things they're blaming.

Mari sits on the pavement, legs crossed, her body drained of fury, feeling as empty as she's ever felt. Conor is walking in circles around her, opening and closing his fingers. It's a heartbreaking dance. He's a satellite, an unheavenly moon circling what is now the center of his life, the gravitational pull of his adopted sister, the one person keeping him from spinning out into space. Mari watches his shadow as it circles around her, and then it stops, suddenly, in the path of the light, eclipsing her own shadow so that their shadows merge as one.

"I made a mistake," Conor says. "It was a mistake. My zipper wouldn't open and I made a mistake."

"I know," Mari said. "It's okay."

"It has to be okay...because it is. Whatever it is, is okay," Conor reasons in his own bizarre fashion. Somehow he's right, though Mari has no idea what being okay means to him.

"I'm hungry," Conor says.

"So am I," Mari responds. "In fact, I'm hungrier. I'm the hungriest."

"No, I'm the hungriest," Conor says.

"This time I'm the hungriest," Mari says, baiting Conor.

"I'm the hungriest," Conor says.

"I'm the hungriest."

"We're both the hungriest!" Conor announces. "We're both the hungriest of all."

"Okay," Mari says, "we're both the hungriest."

"The hungriest brother and sister in the universe," Conor says. And he means it.

Mari stands up and Conor steps toward her until he's only a foot away—the closest he ever gets intentionally to anyone. Mari reaches out for the back of his head and gives it a slight pull, and Conor leans forward. Then, of his own will, he buries his face in her neck, under her chin, and they stand there.

"I can't climb in the toilet," Conor whispers.

"Neither can I," Mari says.

"I would get sick if I climbed in the toilet."

"Probably."

"Definitely. Fecal coliform is a bad vector for disease."

Mari has only a vague idea what he is talking about—some tidbit of information about crap he picked up somewhere that has lodged in his enormous brain.

After fifteen seconds Conor lifts his head and looks around. Mari does too. Now that she's empty of hope, she observes everything without judgment. She looks at the car, filled with gas, the engine still ticking as it cools down from thousands of miles of driving.

The car is useless now. It's still parked by the pump and it will attract attention. She hasn't seen an attendant—maybe someone will come in the morning. If Mari and Conor stand around by the car, eventually a state policeman will find them and they'll be taken away, probably separated. If they hitchhike, their chances of getting a ride are slim, especially in the dark, and the chances of getting caught would be even higher.

Two hundred miles is too far to walk.

Mari goes to the car, leans in to the driver's side, and pops the trunk. She takes out the two sleeping bags, her backpack, and their duffles. Conor crawls into the back seat and emerges with *Astronomy: A Beginner's Guide to the Universe* clutched to his chest with both arms.

Maybe it will protect him from something.

Mari goes around to the passenger side and pulls out the Gulls CD that is still halfway inserted into the player. She slips it into her back pocket, then slides across the seat and fumbles through the glove compartment until she finds a scrap of paper and a pen. She writes a note. *Car broken. Will be back in morning.* Maybe this will buy them a little time. She climbs out of the car, slips the note under the wiper, locks all the doors, then shuts the driver's door. She checks the handles. All the doors are locked.

"Come on. Let's sit over there."

She leads Conor away from the gas pumps and portable toilets toward a small outbuilding to the side of the closed food court and restrooms, out of the glare of the streetlights. She drags the sleeping bags and pads, and Conor cradles his book. Her eyes grow accustomed to the dark and she finds a small grassy spot by the little shed. She unrolls the sleeping bags over the pads and sits down.

"What are you doing?" Conor asks, joining her.

"Waiting for a ride," she says.

"Who's picking us up?" he asks, as if this is a real possibility.

"I don't know yet. The right person."

"Who is the right person?"

"I don't know."

"Do you mean a stranger?" Conor is beginning to go on red alert. "Are we going to ride with a stranger?"

"Only a good stranger," Mari says.

They sit there in silence for a while. Then he asks, "How do you know it's a good stranger?"

"You just know," Mari answers.

Conor's quiet for thirty seconds, then he says, "We are the hungriest."

And then they wait.

Chapter THIRTY-NINE

Over the next hour or two, a few cars do pull into the rest area. Mari sneaks up behind an air pump and examines each person as they get out and fill their tanks. She is only going by feel. No one in too fancy a car, or in too-expensive clothes. No men by themselves.

She's about to approach a couple—she likes the look of the woman who has gone into the portable toilet. She appears to be about forty, dressed down in jeans and a T-shirt and she looks like a mom. After a few minutes the woman comes out of the toilet and Mari is ready to step out of the shadows.

"For Chrissake, Margo!" the man shouts. "Will ya hurry up?" His voice is angry.

Mari slips back into the darkness.

Another hour passes. Conor is lying on his back on the sleeping bag, staring at the stars. Soon she hears a steady breathing and sees he's fallen asleep. She watches him for a moment.

He's good when he's asleep.

A state police car pulls up to the pump behind their old Honda. Mari's heart races. The cop gets out and looks in the car, then walks around it and pulls the note off the windshield. Mari is suddenly afraid they are visible. They should have found a place back in the complete darkness, farther away from any danger of the Official World. Mari slows her breathing and freezes, as still as the night. The cicadas around them start to rise and fall in a thunderous call and she hopes their sound is enough to make her more invisible—sound hiding sight.

The cop looks at the California license plates, then heads over to the restrooms and snack area. He flicks on a flashlight, checks the doors, and starts around the building, sweeping the flashlight back and forth. As he comes closer and closer to them, Mari holds her breath and prays that Conor stays asleep.

By blind luck, they hadn't settled down near the larger building, and the arc of the cop's flashlight beam comes nowhere near them. He disappears, then reappears a couple of minutes later on the far side and heads to his car. Mari can't make out what he is saying on the radio mike, but she hears the crackle of the voice on the other end.

"Please, please, please," she whispers underneath the roar of the summer insects, as if silent prayers are not enough. A bead of sweat trickles down the side of her head from her scalp onto her neck. "Please, no."

"Okay, okay," she hears the cop say. "I'll check back in a little while." Then he slaps a sticker on the side of the car, looks around one more time, and climbs in his cruiser.

As he speeds away from the service area, Mari lets out her breath.

They have to escape before he comes back.

Almost immediately a car pulls in to the far pump. It's not fancy at all—the gas island lights show faded green paint and a dent in a rear fender. Mari gets up and takes a step toward the car. She watches as a woman gets out—she looks like she's in her early thirties, dressed in jeans and a tank top. She's a little heavyset, the tank top rising up over the swell of her wide hips, and her hair is pulled up on top of her head. The woman opens the back door, leans in, and comes out with a barefoot little girl in pajamas.

"Put me down, Mommy," the girl says, kicking her legs. "I have to go!"

"Let's get your sandals on first. There might be glass."

The sleepy little girl argues and whines, but the woman gets something on her feet. "Watch where you're stepping," she says, setting her daughter down on the pavement. The girl runs ahead toward the toilets, the mom trudging along behind. The girl can't reach the handle of the door, so the mom opens it for her. Once again she picks her up.

"Put me down! I can go myself!"

"Let me put you on the seat," the woman says, "I don't want you standing where someone peed."

The door stays open and the woman waits for the girl, then lifts her over to the pavement. "You stay right here. Mommy's gotta go." With the door still open, the woman disappears inside. The girl, wide awake now, dances around on the concrete, skipping sideways in a circle around some imaginary fairy ring.

The woman steps out of the toilet and shuts the door.

Mari knows this is it.

She takes a step out of the shadows, about twenty yards away from them. She doesn't want to scare them.

"Excuse me," she calls.

The woman turns quickly, instinctively putting her arm across the girl's chest and pulling her close.

"I'm over here." Mari steps out of the shadow of the building and into the light. "I'm sorry. I didn't mean to scare you."

She sees the woman's hold on the girl loosen a little.

"What are you doin'? What do you want?"

It suddenly dawns on Mari. The voice sounds like her mom's. This woman must have grown up around Boston too. Inexplicably, Mari feels encouraged, as if any woman from Boston would understand her plight.

"I...I need some help," Mari says. "I don't know what to do."

Has Mari ever said it that clearly to anyone? Has she ever

admitted she has no answers? Even with the biker, she'd told him only what she needed at that particular moment. But now she has given herself up to the universe, to this person she doesn't know.

The woman stands there staring at her, then glances around to see if there's anyone else. She looks back toward the gas pumps.

"Is that your car?"

"Uh-huh. We lost the keys."

"We?"

"My brother—he's sleeping over there."

"How could you friggin' lose the keys? You're just fillin' up the tank, for God's sake."

Omigod, Mari thinks, that's exactly what her mom would say. She takes another step closer.

"My brother dropped them down the toilet. He didn't mean to, but—"

"Seriously? Friggin' seriously?"

Mari nods.

"Holy shit, excuse my French. That is a whole pile of trouble."

And Mari ventures closer to the woman, closer to the girl looking up at her. The girl's eyes are big round plates, staring at this apparition.

"It's more than that," Mari says.

"How much more?"

"A lot more." Mari is trying to keep it together. "We need a ride out of here. We have to go to Boston. It's really important. And we need to go now."

The woman looks back at the Honda.

"What about your car?"

"I don't care about the car. We just need to get to my grandma's."

"Pick me up, Mommy," the pajama girl says, raising her arms. The woman lifts the little girl, who wraps her arms around her mother's neck and looks back inquisitively at Mari.

"Where are you coming from?"

"California," Mari says. She's done making things up. "Los Angeles."

"Holy crap. You drove all the way from Los Angeles?"

"We need to go now," Mari says.

"Let me guess," the woman says. "Before someone catches up with you?"

"Sort of." Mari nods.

"Like the police?"

Mari shrugs. They're not really chasing her, but it sure feels like it.

"Mari! Mari!" a voice calls from the darkness. Conor steps out of the shadows, clutching *The Beginners' Guide to the Universe* under one arm. He half-hops, half-skips in their direction, wagging his head back and forth.

"That's your brother?" the woman asks Mari.

"Yeah. He's autistic," Mari says. She hates the label—it's not who he is, but she only has a couple of seconds to make her case. "It's like he kind of lives in his own world. He's a little different, but he's okay. His name is Conor."

Before the woman can respond, Conor moves closer. He looks at the woman and the kid, then asks Mari, "Who are they? Are they the good strangers who are giving us a ride?"

For a moment no one speaks. They all stand there in a little triangle beneath the lights of the service area, the buzz of the late-summer insects in the bushes, the sound of engines and tires on the interstate. A hot breeze blows across the pavement, sending an empty paper cup rolling by their feet.

Now. Now you say it. Please.

"Yes, we are, Conor," the woman says. "Get your stuff and let's go."

Chapter FORTY

Conor won't budge.

"I'm telling you, it's okay." Mari is begging him now. "Conor, please. We have to go."

"How do we know these are the right people?" he asks, staring at the ground.

"I promise you they are."

Conor shakes his head.

"Mommy, let's go." The little girl is growing skittish now too. The more Conor resists, the less sure she is that she wants him in their car.

Mari looks with pleading eyes at the girl's mother.

"Is that an astronomy book?" the woman asks.

Conor shoots her a quick glance but doesn't answer.

"It looks like a big one," the woman offers.

Mari can see the wheels in Conor's mind spinning, and she holds her breath.

"You must like the stars," the woman says.

"We saw the eclipse." Conor looks straight up, as if the sun and moon are still together overhead.

"Wicked awesome," the woman says.

"Mommy?" the girl whines. Her mother shushes her.

The bugs are calling. Tires are humming on the highway.

"Have you ever been to the planetarium at the Museum of Science in Boston?" the woman asks Conor.

"No." He pauses, then decides to say more. "I've never been to a planetarium. The Hayden Planetarium is at the American Museum of Natural History in New York."

"The one at the Museum of Science is amaaaazing," the woman says. The little girl is watching Conor closely now.

He doesn't respond. Mari can sense that he's struggling here—he's outside of his comfort zone.

The woman holds the planetarium out like a big piece of chocolate cake. Or maybe an Edith's Original Barbecue Potato Chip. "I guess if you're going to live in Boston, you'll probably see it. A lot."

After another moment of silence, Conor heads back into the darkness. But he's not running—he's on a mission. In thirty seconds he returns, dragging the sleeping bags and pads. He walks over to the woman's car and stands at the door, waiting.

"Evidently, we're going," she says.

"I guess so," Mari answers.

Her name is Trish. Her daughter is Sabrina. They're driving to see Trish's mother in Malden, Massachusetts.

That's all she says, but Mari knows there's more, because the car is stuffed to the gills. They have to squeeze the sleeping bags behind the back seat. Mari is holding her duffle in the front seat, and Conor is wedged in the back in a little squirrel's nest of bags and clothes and bed linens and kids' toys. He had wanted to take the dog crate, but it was locked in the Honda. The space he climbed into, right behind Mari, is cozier and tighter than the crate, though, and Mari senses he feels safe there. Conor is still clutching his astronomy book—Mari figures his desire for the planetarium is just a little bit larger than his uneasiness with strangers.

Ten minutes later she cranes her head around and sees that both Conor and Sabrina have fallen asleep.

Trish drives for a little while without speaking. Mari sneaks a glance at the woman and sees a sadness at the edges of her eyes. Mari senses a weariness in the way her hands are draped over the steering wheel, in the way she takes a deep breath, then lets it out slowly, like she's trying to rid herself of something that has been buried deep inside her. But Mari sees the toughness, too. The kind of toughness her mom had.

"My mom died," Mari says suddenly.

It's quiet for minute, then Trish says, "Well, that sucks."

That's exactly what it does. Her mom died and it sucks.

"I was adopted," Mari adds.

When Trish doesn't say anything, Mari sneaks another

sideways glance at her. Trish senses it and gives Mari a quick look, then turns back to the windshield.

"I was in foster care before. I don't want to go back."

Trish nods. "Jesus, I don't blame you."

"I'm only fifteen." Again, Mari looks to see Trish's reaction, and again the woman just nods.

Mari lets her story trickle out one sentence at a time. She pauses after each sentence to see if it's accepted, and each time, Trish nods. With each nod, Trish passes a test, and Mari tells a little more.

The words come more freely as they drive through the night. Then, finally, Mari is storytelling—leaning toward Trish, using her hands and body to emphasize what she's been through and what she's seen. She tells about the foster homes, Maggie Custer and the attack of the wooden spoon, the years with Kevin and Stef, and the arrival of her brother.

She slows down as she reaches the day when her mom was taken to the hospital.

Was that less than a week ago?

Mari is quiet for a long moment, thinking about the last few days. Then she picks up her story again, describing Dennis's words during the phone call in the hospital and the hurried escape to Target for the Honda. When she gets to the parts about Conor barking from the dog crate in the carport and about knocking over Nosy Rosie Cosamini's reflecting ball, Trish laughs out loud.

When Mari speaks the words, when someone hears her stories, they seem to become more real. Everything that happened will stay in the world—not just in her memory, but also in someone else's.

Trish snorts out another laugh as Mari describes throwing Sky's backpack down on the entrance ramp. "You are wicked crazy!" she says in admiration. "I wish I had your guts."

Mari smiles. "Wicked" is a word her mom used, and it had taken Mari a while to realize it didn't mean "bad"—it was a Boston way of ratcheting things up a notch.

Wicked crazy.

Wicked good.

Wicked strong.

Mari pulls the CD out of the back pocket of her shorts, rubs it clean with the tail of her T-shirt, and asks if she can put it into the player.

Trish gestures for her to go ahead.

Mari slips in the CD and the first notes play.

"Omigod," says Trish. "It's the Gulls." Trish reaches over and turns up the volume on the player.

"Do you know this CD?" Mari asks. "It was one of my mom's."

"God, I loved this band. I haven't heard this in a million years."

"My mom loved them too."

Trish nods. There's nothing more to say. But when the song "I Don't Belong to You" comes on, Mari can feel the electricity in the car, fueled by the band's energy. She looks at Trish and sees her mouthing the lyrics: *Don't tell me what to do, I don't belong to you.* And when the song is over, without a word, she pushes the button to hear it again.

"Oh man," Trish says under her breath.

The car floats through the universe, lifted by the music in the night. They're each alone in their separate thoughts, but together somehow.

"So you're going to your mom's for a visit?" Mari finally asks, although she knows it's not as simple as that. You don't stuff a car full of bed linens and suitcases and toys for a little visit to your mom's.

"We're going to stay for a while," Trish says. "Till we figure things out."

So now it's Trish's turn. First a sentence, then another and another until the sentences string together into a story. Mari tries to be supportive, like Trish has been for her, nodding and assenting, agreeing with her and who she is.

This story is about a husband who turns into someone the wife no longer recognizes.

Trish, like Mari, becomes more and more animated in the telling. "Hitting me is one thing," she finishes. "But hitting Sabrina is another. We weren't safe. So I got out."

"Yeah," Mari says, which is all she feels capable of saying. Listening is the only way Mari knows to show she cares.

There's a reciprocity here—something offered and something returned. One story begets another. One story isn't done until the next one is shared, and that's what Trish and

Mari do as the Gulls sing to both of them. Mari wonders what it would be like to have an older sister—someone who's been through it before you. Someone who has your back.

"Mommy," Sabrina calls from the back of the car. "I'm cold."

"Hold on a little while, pumpkin," Trish answers. "The blankets are all packed away."

"Wait," Mari says. She unzips the duffle on her lap and feels around for the wool of the reindeer sweater. She pulls it out and hands it back to Sabrina.

"It has reindeers on it," Mari says. "You can use it like a blanket."

"Like Santa's reindeers?" Sabrina asks.

"Just like them," Mari answers. "I got it from my grandmother, but it's too small for me. So you can have it."

"What do you say, Sabrina?" Trish asks.

"Thank you!" Sabrina warbles. She snuggles into the sweater and falls back asleep.

Chapter FORTY-ONE

Mari looks at the clock on the dashboard. It's 4:32 in the morning and she's drowsy, but she doesn't want to go to sleep. She wants to keep going, keep talking. She's safe here. Why go anywhere else?

They're in Massachusetts now—she didn't notice when that happened. She sees a sign for Springfield. They are coming closer and closer to the end. It's as if the car isn't really moving, but rather the earth is turning under the wheels of the car, pulling her closer and closer to where she is headed. She doesn't really want to think about what might happen. She doesn't want to think that the door might not open. That Nana won't be there. That she won't care or will still be angry. Right now Mari can't bear the thought of anyone being angry with her, and she feels an anger rising up in her. After all this, she doesn't deserve anyone's anger.

But then she thinks, *I do deserve it.*

"I bet your grandmother will be happy to see you," Trish says out of the blue. Or maybe because Mari's brain waves wafted across the car and into Trish's own consciousness.

"I don't know," Mari says. "Maybe not."

"Why not?"

So there's one more story to tell. As she tells it, it sounds even worse. About getting pissed off and taking the opal brooch out of Nana's bag and grabbing a hammer—a friggin' hammer!—and smashing her grandmother's beloved pin right in front of her because she wants to hurt her. And she does hurt her. Horribly.

But it was what she said that hurt her grandmother the most.

Mari understands now, more than before, how horrible it was, because she's a different person than the one who hammered the opal into pieces. She's a person who can see that what she does affects other people.

Now Mari can look back at the eleven-year-old with understanding. And she realizes there's still a price to pay. She just doesn't know what it is or if whatever she has to pay it with will be enough.

At the end of the story, Trish asks, "So you haven't talked to her since?"

Mari shakes her head and tells Trish that after that, Nana never answered or returned calls from her mom.

"Nothing?" Trish asks.

"Nothing," Mari answers. "Once, I asked her if my grandmother was still mad."

"What did she say?" Trish asks.

Mari looks out the window ahead, to where the sky is lightening in the east.

"She said there's some things you can fix, and some you can't."

And then it's quiet for a while.

Trish points to a green highway mileage sign that says "Boston 23."

"I'm going to take you to Lynn," she says. "It's not far out of my way."

"It's okay," Mari says. "You need to get to your mom's. I'll figure something out from there."

"How much money do you have?"

"Enough." Which is a lie. "It's okay. I got this far."

"I know it's okay," Trish says. "Which is why I'm going to take you to Lynn."

"You don't have to," Mari protests.

"Too bad for you, because I am," Trish responds. She gives Mari a quick smile and looks back at the road.

There's a minute or two of quiet, and then Trish speaks up again. "Look, Mari. I'm the last person who has the right to say this, but you can't make someone forgive you. You can only ask that they do. The rest is up to them."

Mari nods, but doesn't say anything.

"And one more thing, then I'll shut up. There were three people there, and it took all of you to make it happen. And I don't want to be too hard on the other ones, but you were not the grown-up. You were just a kid."

Mari nods and swallows.

They drive another five minutes. The sun is rising and the

traffic is building up as the highway goes from four to six to eight lanes.

"Where are we?" Conor says, waking up in the back seat. "I have to pee."

"It's only a little farther," Mari says. "Just try to hold it."

"And I'm hungry," Conor adds. "The hungriest."

"No," says Mari. "I'm the hungriest."

"We're both the hungriest," Conor responds. "We're the hungriest brother and sister."

"I'm hungrier than you are," Trish says, joining in the game.

"No, you're not," Conor says. "It's us. It's not even close."

Mari and Trish laugh.

Conor says, "It's not funny."

But it is. And then a little voice pipes up from the other side of the back seat. "I'm hungriest too."

"No, you're not," Conor says. "You have to have a sister to be the hungriest."

Conor's World. It will last forever. It's not something you can fix. It's something that is.

As they drive through Boston, the traffic grows heavier. The sun shines on a huge building, its light reflecting on the dark blue windows.

"Conor," Mari says. "What's Nana's address?"

"Forty-two Mill Street, Lynn, Massachusetts, 01902."

"Impressive," Trish says, handing Mari her phone.

Mari punches in the address and watches the map come up with the red marker hovering over Nana's house.

They drive through a tunnel beneath the city, then out onto a bridge that arcs grandly and promises something wonderful on the other side. Its spine of white cables spins out over the water that glimmers and sparkles in the early morning light.

Mari thinks about what to say to Nana. How to ask. How to get the answer she wants. The answer she and Conor need. A simple, one word answer.

Suddenly she's overcome with doubt. Her mind runs in circles.

This is all a horrible mistake. I should not have done this. What will I do with Conor when Nana won't take us in? I can survive in a foster home for a while. In three years I'll be done with it—they can't keep me after that. I'll be a grown-up and I'll do what I want.

But what about my brother? Would he survive until I could come back for him?

He'll have to.

And I have to do this alone.

I don't need anyone's help.

Trish exits the highway and turns left onto a residential street. Mari decides she's going to get out now and have Trish take Conor on to Nana's house. If Nana is mad at her, maybe she'll take just Conor.

But Mari doesn't say or do anything.

"Almost there," Trish says.

"Right at the next corner," Mari says, her heart in her throat. Trish makes the turn.

No! No! I need to get out of the car!

But Mari hears herself saying, "Turn left here at the school."

Trish turns. Then there's another left, and another right. Mari keeps giving the directions in spite of herself, until they turn onto Mill Street.

"Stop!" Mari says.

Trish puts on the brakes. "Right here?" she asks. "Is this the house?" She cranes her neck, looking at the houses on the right and left.

It's not too late. I can still get out.

Mari looks down the street at the houses and lawns and trees. But it's not what she sees that matters right now. It's what she hears.

She hears her mom. Her real mom. Stef. The one who took her in and loved her. *"Who's the grown-up?"*

All those times her mom had asked that, she had meant Mari. Mari was supposed to be the grown-up. But her mom was wrong. Mari shouldn't have to be the grown-up. She doesn't even want to be a grown-up. Not yet.

She does need someone to care for her.

She needs Nana.

"No," Mari says. "Up just a little farther."

Trish guides the car slowly down the street. Past a house with a white picket fence. Past a three-story house with laundry hanging on a line out of the second floor.

"Here," Mari says. She remembers the house. A brown shingled roof over a screened and windowed sun porch, where she slept. She can almost smell the musty comforter she'd snuggled under. The door is to the left of the porch.

"This is it," Mari says.

"The number is over the door," Conor says. "Forty-two."

Trish pulls to the curb and turns off the ignition. The engine ticks, cooling down.

Mari looks up at the steps, at the storm door. The place is clean and neat. She remembers Nana sweeping the steps every morning.

"Do you want me to come with you?" Trish asks.

"No," Mari says. "We're good. Thank you for everything." She reaches for the door handle.

"Wait." Trish pushes the eject button on the stereo and holds the Gulls CD out to Mari. "Don't forget this."

Mari reaches for it, but then pulls her hand back. "No," she says. "I want you to have it."

"I can't," Trish says.

"Yes, you can," Mari answers, nodding. "You have to."

Trish shakes her head, then grabs a piece of paper lying on the floor of the car and scribbles down a number. "You can always call me. I'll come."

Mari folds the note and slips it into her front pocket. "It's okay," she says, then frowns at how stupid that sounds. She thinks for a moment that maybe they could go with Trish to Malden, that they wouldn't be a bother.

But they *would* be a bother. People are a bother. And she and Conor are a particular kind of bother.

"Call me either way," Trish says. "I just want to hear from you."

Conor opens his door first, and Mari pushes hers open. She's not the grown-up. But she's still the big sister.

"We need our sleeping bags," Conor says. "And I'm hungry. And I have to pee." He pulls the bags and mats out of the car.

Mari climbs out, then turns and looks at Trish. "Thanks again," she says.

"No problem," Trish says.

"You can go," Mari says.

"I'll just stay here a minute."

Mari walks up the short sidewalk to the three steps leading to the front door. Conor follows, dragging the sleeping bags behind him. A bird chirps in a tree overhead.

Before Mari can change her mind, she reaches out and pushes the doorbell. She doesn't hear a ring. She waits a few seconds, then pushes the bell again. No footsteps. No sound of a lock being unlocked or a door opening.

Her courage fails her. She turns and sees Trish bending over to look out the passenger window. She hears Sabrina whining in the back that she's hungry.

"What are you doing?" Conor asks.

"Let's go," Mari says. "Nobody's home."

But Conor is standing in her way. "That's dumb," he says.

"Let's go," she says again. She doesn't want to push him, but she will.

"The doorbell doesn't work," Conor says. "You can't hear it ringing." He pulls open the storm door and knocks loudly. "Nana! Nana! Open up! It's Conor! Let us in! I have to pee."

Mari wants to run. She looks back toward the street. Trish is motioning to Mari to turn around.

And so Mari turns to face the door.

"Nana!" Conor shouts. "It's us! Me and Mari! You have to open up."

Mari hears a bolt unlock. The door opens. A woman looks down at them from the entranceway. She puts her hand to her throat, and then spreads it out across the left side of her chest, as if she were trying to feel the beat of her heart.

"Nana," Mari blurts out. "I'm sorry."

The old woman's bottom lip trembles and a tentative smile opens her mouth.

"Oh, my darlings," she says. "I was hoping you would come."

END

Acknowledgments

I often tell young people when I talk about being an author, "There is the story in the book, and the story of the book." If *Now You Say Yes* is an odyssey, so is the story of its coming into being, and it had the help of dozens people along its journey into your hands. It was a long, joyous, and sometimes very difficult trip. I owe thanks to many.

First, to my niece Tess Stewart, the fourteen-year old (at the time) from Los Angeles who helped me hatch the story one day at the kitchen table, and to her mom, Leslie Stewart, exemplary LAUSD teacher who told me early on it was good.

Thanks to Dr. Barry Prizant for his early advice and comments on the nature and challenges of Autism Spectrum

Disorder (ASD). His encouragement kept me on course. I highly recommend his book, *Uniquely Human: A Different Way of Seeing Autism.*

Thanks to the Correia family, David, Cathy, Lucas, and especially Matthew, who continue to show me a beautiful way to approach ASD.

To the friends who helped me on my own trip following Mari and Conor's route, and were also early readers—Ellen Dinerman, Berkley Hudson, Milbre Burch, and Ellen Munds. To R.E.M. and *Automatic for the People*, a great recording that isn't in the book, but played a huge part in developing Mari and Conor's soundtrack.

To all the readers who provided support and a careful reading: David Kranes, lifelong friend, mentor and cheerleader; Jane Murphy, reader extraordinaire with a gimlet eye; Meaghan Lenihan, who knows the middle school reader's mind; Liliah Carey, Psy.D., for her reading and insights about adoption and at-risk youth.

Thanks to Anne Hoppe for friendship and advice; to the other three Directions—Clare Murphy, Kevin Kling, and Dovie

Thomason—for their ears, shoulders, hearts, and minds; and to Andy Offut Irwin for support and contacts.

To the thousands of students in schools across the country who listened to me talk about the story before anything had been written down—thanks for their enthusiasm and penetrating questions about how kids could do what Mari and Conor did, and their problem-solving capabilities. Stories are best first spoken out loud and I'm lucky to have an audience in school classrooms and assemblies.

To Vicky Holifield, my loyal and honest editor and compatriot—this book is a team project, even if it's only my name on the cover. And to Margaret Quinlin for her vision of what a publishing company can be, and all the other folks at Peachtree who share in that mission. Many, many thanks.

To my sons, Noah and Dylan, who both have an incredible understanding of story. And of course, as in the dedication, to my wife Debbie Block—my first listener and reader, and honorary godmother of Conor and Mari. I wouldn't be who I am without her.

Obviously, this is a work of imagination and an author

necessarily goes out on a limb, making guesses about the way things are or might be. Especially in the area of ASD and questions of identity for young people in the foster care system, there is much to get wrong and misunderstand. If there are oversights or errors in portrayal, those faults are mine and no one else's. That said, I, for the moment, know I've done the best that I can to put myself in someone else's shoes. Which is what story is all about.

—B. H.

About the author

Bill Harley is a two-time Grammy Award-winning storyteller, musician, and writer who has been writing and performing for kids and families for more than forty years. He is the author of several highly acclaimed picture books and novels for middle readers, including *Night of the Spadefoot Toads* and the popular Charley Bumpers series. He lives in Massachusetts.